SEVEN

the oldest was a
youngest, fifteen.

THEY HAD NAMES

Buck Burnett, Miller Nalls, Little Bit
Luckett, Todo MacLean, Eubank Buell,
Willy Bill Beardan, J. C. (Julius Caesar)
Sutton. But now, one hundred years later,
who remembers them?

THEY FOUGHT FOR A LOST CAUSE

but they didn't know that war is hell and
that shining courage must become
dogged endurance, that the man on the
horse had better get down in the mud
when the Minie balls start whistling . . .

WILL HENRY TELLS THE STORY OF
THESE SEVEN IN HIS ACTION-PACKED,
ADVENTURE-FILLED NOVEL OF THE OLD
WEST IN THE CIVIL WAR—**JOURNEY TO
SHILOH**

Books by Will Henry

❧ NO SURVIVORS

❧ PILLARS OF THE SKY

❧ THE FOURTH HORSEMAN

❧ THE RAIDERS

❧ WHO RIDES WITH WYATT

❧ THE NORTH STAR

❧ THE RECKONING AT YANKEE FLAT

❧ FROM WHERE THE SUN NOW STANDS

❧ SEVEN MEN AT MIMBRES SPRING

❧ THE FELEEN BRAND

❧ Published by Bantam Books

JOURNEY TO
SHILOH
WILL HENRY

BANTAM BOOKS NEW YORK

JOURNEY TO SHILOH

*A Bantam Book / published by arrangement with
Random House, Inc.*

PRINTING HISTORY

*Random House edition published October 1960
Bantam edition published April 1963*

*Bantam Books are published by Bantam Books, Inc. Its trade-mark,
consisting of the words "Bantam Books" and the portrayal of a
bantam, is registered in the United States Patent Office and in other
countries. Marca Registrada. Printed in the United States of Amer-
ica. Bantam Books, Inc., 271 Madison Ave., New York 16, N. Y.*

FOR JACK SCHAEFER

MY FRIEND

Contents

1 The Captain

THEY CAME TO THE CROSSING and put their ponies into its shallows. The little horses plunged their dusty muzzles into the green water. They were eager to drink, yet not greedy. They took nice care, after the manner of true Spanish *mesteños*, both as to the amount of water consumed and the measure of time employed in consuming it. Their riders, too, took care. They were Western men, watchful, far-eyed, eternally on guard against the stillness around them. No ounce of the fat of easy living showed among the seven of them. Their physical spareness was matched by the economy of their conversation.

"How far we come, you figure?" said one.

"A decent piece," estimated another.

"This here's the Paint Rock Crossing of the Concho," volunteered a third.

"That would make it right on forty miles," guessed the fourth.

"Give or take ten minutes' ride," agreed the fifth.

The last two men said nothing. They were not the talking but the listening and the looking kind.

The idle tongue of the river gossiped briefly during the human lull. Downstream a she-fox, her hunting disturbed, barked her resentment of the intruders. Off to the north a dog-coyote, sampling the tainted wind from the crossing, replied to the vixen's complaint. After that there were only the sounds of the water again. Presently the mustangs raised their heads.

"What do you say, Buck?" asked the sixth man.

His companion stood in his stirrups. He peered eastward across the Concho, then squinted thoughtfully back into the late sun. Satisfied, he nodded quickly.

"We come far enough for one day, Miller. Tell Eubie and Willy Bill to scout back a ways. Rest of us will cross on over and make camp."

Miller Nalls returned the nod admiringly. It was like Buck Burnet to have you tell the others for him when he wasn't

1

twenty feet from them himself. Buck was simply one of those natural-born few who took charge with never a thought that it should be any other way. Miller liked that in Buck. It gave him confidence.

"Eubie," he said, "you and Willy Bill circle back and make sure we ain't picked up any company. Buck says we come far enough for one day."

"Suits me," said ordinary soldier Eubank Buell. "You game, Willy Bill?"

"As a bear-dog," claimed fellow enlisted man W.B. Bearden. "Let's ramble."

They rode off along the river, one up it, one down. Shortly they swung inland, pinching together on the trail their party had made into Paint Rock Crossing. Out over the darkening prairie nothing moved saved the things which should: a bull-bat fluttering out to begin its evening bug hunt; a tiny cactus owl floating from her spiny perch upon the same business; a wary Texas red wolf cocking his head at the motionless riders from a nearby ridge.

Trading half a dozen words the two scouts turned their mounts for the Concho. Ordinarily it did not pay to camp at this place, since it was a favorite watering spot for the Comanche bands moving east to horse-raid in the settlements. But with Buck Burnet in charge no one needed to give a second thought to campsites or Comanches. Buck knew what he was doing. He was a boy who would have a go at skinning a live bobcat barehanded. At the same time he would not do it that way if he could find a pair of stout gloves. That was what gave people such a sense of trust in him. He was always thinking. Always watching.

While his comrades shared these thoughts of him Buck Burnet went about deserving them. He ordered the supper fire laid while it was yet late day. He saw to it that the small flame was fed with driftwood, so dry its smoke would not dirty the air over the next rise. And he had Willy Bill and Eubie go to the river and bring water so that the fire's last coals could be drowned before full darkness fell. In these knowing ways he had his camp secure and his men in their blankets by gray twilight.

To say the latter were in their blankets was not to say they were asleep. Naturally they were not. This was very high adventure and they were very young men.

Buck himself was but seventeen. Miller Nalls, the friend of his boyhood, was the eldest of the troop at twenty. Of the others Little Bit Luckett was the baby at fifteen. Todo MacLean, Little Bit's self-elected nursemaid, was his senior by one year. Scarcely turned seventeen were fun-loving Eubie

Buell and "game as a bear-dog" Willy Bill Bearden. The last of them was sullenly handsome Julius Caesar Sutton, at eighteen the fastest hand with a Colt's revolver the Concho side of San Antonio, and a boy who would quickly prove it to any fool persisting in calling him by his given name rather than his initials, J.C.

Buck shook his head, lay watching the stars come out. He listened to the river slide rustlingly by, thought some more about who they were, why they were here, where they were going.

They were all Concho County boys except J.C., whose folks lived south of the river in Menard County. J.C. had been up visiting the Lucketts, who were kinfolk, when the grand idea to organize the troop had seized Buck and he had subsequently got the others excited enough to throw in with him. They called themselves the Concho County Comanches. Now that they were on their way, however, a man could not but wonder what J.C. and the rest were thinking of themselves and their decision. Not that it mattered, of course. It was a shade late for second guessing.

It was in fact the twelfth of March, 1862. The fighting back East was barely a month shy of one year old and a boy could only pray it would last until he and his friends might get there. *There* was all the way to Richmond, Virginia. And what Buck and his boys had decided to do was to ride the whole distance to the Confederate capital and humbly offer their services to John Bell Hood's Texas Brigade of the Army of Northern Virginia.

Buck scowled and set his jaw. The red-headed ranch boy felt the pride of the idea arise anew within him. His eyes snapped, his jaw jutted more firmly than ever. He looked out over the starlit Concho and around about him at the blanketed forms of his faithful men and he took a deep and sober oath. He was a Southerner and a soldier. At the head of his Concho County Comanches, Buck Burnet would drive those invading Yankees so far back across the Potomac that the Washington, D.C. boundary line would have to be moved up into the state of Maine.

2   Discipline in the Ranks

THE CONCHO COUNTY COMANCHES, viewed presently, were
the images of their fathers who had chased the real Comanches out of middle Texas in the thirties and forties. They
were wild and unwashed, wore their hair long, their tempers
short. They dressed in leather flayed from a whitetail buck
or Spanish longhorn steer. They had learned to ride at two,
shoot at four, scalp at twelve, squaw at sixteen. There was
nothing in the West Texas world they did not know about
horses, cattle, or Kwahadi Indians. There was, similarly,
nothing in the East Texas settlements they were not eager to
learn about fancy-fronted saloons and fair-skinned women.
Most of Buck's boys had never seen a grown white girl.
Indian and Mexican girls they knew about, but those of their
own race, no. The lack, moreover, was certain to make
trouble in Dallas, just ahead now. Young hell had been building up in them for too long a time.

They had come east, following the stageline through Big
Spring and Palo Pinto to Fort Worth. The smaller settlements had presented no problem. But Fort Worth was another matter. There the lot of them had drawn a night in
jail for jeopardizing the peace of the community. It was
Little Bit's backing of Todo MacLean's $250 bet with a
faro dealer in the Traildriver's Saloon that Little Bit could
jump his horse over three poker tables set end-to-end, which
had started off the evening. Given this advantage, inherent
West Texas enthusiasm had bloomed like a cactus rose, con-
stitutional vigor supplying whatever inventive talent may have
been lacking among the fortified Comanches.

Still, what could a reasonable leader expect? It had been
a chanceful, dusty ride from Concho County and a man
had to stand back and give his boys a little room to let
down. Besides, Little Bit had made the jump and the wager
money was welcome as late summer rain. Now, though, as
they drew near Dallas, that money was only adding to the
main worry.

Buck shook his shaggy red head. He hadn't expected it to
be like this. He was being called upon to behave more like
a foster mother than a captain in charge of troops. No
matter, though. Once a man had taken on a job, he was

4

obligated to see it through. There was but one real question: granted the certainty of too much whiskey and too many women waiting ahead, how was he to go about maneuvering his command past the enemy with minimum casualties?

Poor Buck wound up talking to the empty space between the ears of his steeldust gelding. By-and-by, along about dusk, they came to where they could see the first lights of Dallas winking at them from far across the murky plain, and Buck decided he would hold up and have a word with his boys.

The word did not go down so well with J.C. All the others could see Buck's point about avoiding Dallas, and actually J.C. could see it, too. But he was the kind who spent his life as though it were Mexican money and in danger of being no good if he kept it long enough for the green ink to dry. He so expressed himself to Buck.

"Likely," he said, "you can sell that brand of bull to the rest. Me, I figure to keep right on rolling my own. Any arguments?"

Buck watched him carefully.

"What you meaning to say, J.C.?" he asked.

"I'm meaning to say," answered the Menard County boy, "that if you and the others want to steer clear of Dallas, you go to it. I'm going right smack through the middle of town, myself."

"You are?" said Buck uncertainly.

"I am," said J.C. Sutton.

They had all dismounted to loosen cinches and let their ponies cool out while Buck talked. As was normal with prairie boys they had squatted on their heels to listen. Now they grew whisper-quiet as Buck and J.C. came to a stand looking one another in the eye at somewhere around six feet three or four inches off the ground.

Eubie Buell winced and said out of the corner of his mouth to his friend Willy Bill, "My old daddy used to allow that if you wanted to collect stuffing for a featherbed you put two young cock birds in the same pen of pullets and stood back with your cotton sack spread wide. He guaranteed you a hotelful of ticking fodder in five minutes."

Willy Bill bobbed his head solemnly.

"My daddy put it that it took only two growls and a back-leg scratch to turn a sociable tail-sniffing into a first-class dogfight," he replied.

"By damn," said Eubie, "that's good! Now I reckon we've had our two growls and are only waiting for the leg-scrape."

"Yes," agreed Willy Bill, "and yonder she comes."

He was correct and it was J.C. Sutton doing the scraping.

"Buck," said the dark-haired youth, "I done told you I was going through the middle of Dallas. Now you had best back off and give me the room to get started."

He did not make any visible move with his right hand but suddenly there it was brushing the butt of his revolver. Buck drifted back a step, giving him the requested passing room for his pony. J.C. gave him a cold look, and began moving proud and tough toward his mount.

As far as he went he looked very impressive, but he only went as far as abreast of Buck Burnet. The crack of the latter's fist on his jaw sounded like a chunk of dry cedar being broken across the bunkhouse stove. J.C. stiffened, melted at the knees, went down into the dirt of the Dallas road. He was still pointed toward his pony but he was not going to get to him under his own power that evening. When Buck said quietly, "Pick him up and put him across his paint, I mean to see he goes through Dallas like he wanted," no one argued the order. Little Bit caught up J.C.'s spotted pony and his partner Todo scooped up the unconscious youth and deposited him across the saddle. Todo asked Buck if they should tie J.C. so he wouldn't fall off and Buck answered no, that he appeared to be hanging just right the way he was.

So that was the way in which Julius Caesar Sutton went through Dallas, head and arms flopping down one stirrup fender, stovepipe boots and Sonora spurs down the other. He did not mind the trip and set a good example to the other boys with his quiet manners. As for the latter, they were most soberingly reconvinced that Buck Burnet was the man for captain, the proper bearing of their march through town demonstrating the new degree of loyalty in a heartening way.

One hundred and seventy-five miles ahead rolled the Red River of Texas. On its shores waited Shreveport, first foreign city on their line of march.

"We will wet our whistles in Louisiana," said Buck to Miller Nalls riding at his side. "That's a promise."

"Word and hand, Buck?" said the other.

"Word and hand," repeated Buck solemnly.

"I'll tell the boys," grinned Miller, and turned his head and called the good news back softly.

"Suits me," Eubie Buell answered from the rearward darkness. "I'm certain sick of Texas whiskey."

Their leader glanced back at them, and by the time he did, even Eubie Buell's pony was picking its way without any help from its sleeping rider. Buck blinked hard and bit back a yawn of his own. He straightened and smiled a superior small smile. It was largely honest pleasure over his boys having stood behind him and done what he asked of them. But his smile was touched, too, with the least trace of satisfaction that he had marched them all asleep in their saddles while he still remained head high and watchful in his.

"They'll do," he said proudly to Miller Nalls. "They will make soldiers. They will toughen to it. We've a ways to go yet, you'll see, you'll see . . ."

He let it mumble off and Miller, eyeing him a long moment, said, "Sure, Buck, that's right." As he did so he reached over and gathered up the slack reins of his friend's pony and began leading the little steeldust so that he wouldn't stumble and throw Buck Burnet off into the brush.

3 The Second-in-Command

As soon as Buck went to sleep in the saddle Miller began looking for a camp spot. He found a good one. It had a live spring, a maverick clump of cottonwood scrub, a fine stand of prairie hay for the horses. You couldn't beat a place like that in the flat Texas midlands and Miller was proud of himself. Buck could scarcely have done better had he been awake to try. He was still snoring peacefully when Miller lifted him out of the saddle and laid him to rest alongside the others, all of whom had stumbled off their mounts and into their blankets with no more worry for Buck than for their faithful ponies.

Miller pulled and stacked the saddles, turning the little horses free. There was no thought of hobbles or picket ropes. A good Spanish-blood mustang, properly trained and treated, would no more leave his master than would a sheepdog. When morning came they would be there full of tough Texas hay and ready to run a furlong or a fortnight.

The stock turned out, Miller sought his own blankets. He was well pleased, if very weary. It was downright fun being the leader. A person could begin to see why Buck took to it so willingly. Miller thought drowsily that he

would not mind trying it again when the boys would be
awake to watch him.

He awoke with the sun in his eyes and Buck Burnet's
hand on his shoulder.

The others were still asleep and Buck, looking very serious about something, held a warning finger to his lips and
beckoned Miller to come along. Miller got up and followed
him down to the spring branch where Buck had a fire built
and the coffee can bubbling over it.

"Throw some water in your face while I pour you a cup,"
said Buck. "I want to do some talking."

Miller nodded sleepily, got down on his knees alongside
the creek, splashed a scant tablespoon of water faceward,
rumped back up and reached for his coffee tin.

Buck was worried. They had been on the road two weeks,
he said. They had made from ten to sixty miles a day,
averaging thirty. At that rate they would be all summer
reaching Richmond and it was Buck's growing fear they
might never get to Virginia in time to fight. Did Miller
have any good suggestions for getting more miles a day out
of their mustangs without winding them up hot backed
and hoofsplit?

The latter thought it over, then said, yes, why not tie
the hulls down on the little devils hard and fast, hook the
spurshanks under their flankstraps, point them for Louisiana
and fan with a swat of the hat on every jump? Buck considered the idea, decided it covered the subject to suit his
own sentiments. If Miller would go roll out the boys, he
said, he would round up the saddle stock.

4   Delaying Action

IN THE SUCCEEDING DAYS they passed through Kaufman,
Van Zandt, Wood and Upshur Counties into Harrison County,
following the Texas & Pacific's new survey route through
Mendota and Longview, heading for Marshall, Red River and
Shreveport. At Mendota they met the Amon twins and
Ariadne Lassiter, and encountered their first hint that the
war meant different things to different people. It was here,
too, they bid unwilling farewell to an invisible companion of
the spirit, which had marched with them every proud step

of the way from the frontier—their Concho County conception of the word "Texan." For the Far West met the Old South at Mendota and to unschooled ranch boys this was a disquieting experience. It proved, nonetheless, and particularly for Buck Burnet, an exhilarating one.

At Mendota Buck stood upon the edge of a strange new world. Of all the Comanches he alone sensed the element of change for what it was—a truly alien dimension. The others were conscious only of the visual newness. They did not *feel* Mendota as Buck did. Still, the latter could no more describe this deeper awareness, this growing anxiety within, than could his less sensitive companions.

At dusk of a fine day they made camp on the outskirts of an impressive small city on the banks of the Sabine River. As was their custom, they remained a safe distance from the settlement. Buck believed in behaving like soldiers, staying away from the local people and not quartering upon them in any degree. This discipline had worked to avoid trouble with the countryside but it had not fitted the Comanches for the difficulty now facing them, and it had given them many a hungry night upon the prairie when they might otherwise have fed deep and slept like kings merely for the polite asking. As a result they were showing some edge approaching Mendota and Buck was prepared to make certain concessions, provided the right excuse presented itself. This appeared in the form of two town boys about their own ages, twins to judge from their matching blond curls and blue eyes, who showed up at their campfire just as they were heeling down to their dried beef and pinto beans.

The visitors proved such a compelling blend of proper silence, hopeful freckled grins and frankly envious curiosity as to demand of the Comances a Western invitation to "light down and dig in." The town boys seemed surprised by this generosity but came on into the fire's full light, nonetheless. After a bad moment of boot scuffing, they squatted down on their heels in awkward imitation of their hosts' easy postures, accepted their plates with courteous "thank you's," proceeded to "dig in" as directed. For another longish spell it seemed the situation was getting too quiet. The city boys made a show of being busy with their food while the Comanches put on an undue fuss over doing up the supper dishes. Both sides were clearly dying to talk, yet neither appeared able to think of any topic which might do for a starter. Characteristically, it was Eubie Buell who felt he held openers and played them accordingly.

"You all from yonder town?" he asked recklessly.

"Yes, sir," replied one of the boys. "Both of us."

Eubie cocked a narrowed eye at the newcomer.

"You figure that to be funny?" he demanded.

"No, sir," said the boy. "It's the gospel truth."

Eubie looked at the other Comanches, lifted a superior eyebrow and turned back to the city boy.

"That's some town you got there, ain't it?" he said. "What's she called?"

"Mendota," answered the boy, then gestured quickly. "It's all right, I guess, but I'd a heap rather live out where you fellows come from." He stared at the rough leather garb and weather-beaten faces of the Comanches, envy, admiration and perhaps a little apprehension mixing in the wide-eyed appraisal. "Say," he said, "you all are from really way out yonder, aren't you?" He flung an arm wildly westward. "I mean really, *really* way out yonder!"

"We are," replied Buck with his usual dignity. "We're from Concho County. That's about as far yonder as she goes."

"Jings," breathed the boy, "Concho County!" He wheeled on his brother. "You hear that, Cart? They're from Concho County. Imagine it. Why that's past Fort Worth!"

"It's wild out there, isn't it?" said the other boy, Cart, the quiet one, to Buck. "Awful wild, I mean."

"I believe that you could say it is," said Buck. "Providing you wasn't used to it, anyways."

"There's Indians?" persisted Cart. "The warbonnet kind, with horses and scalp belts and such?"

"All you'd want," said Buck, "but nothing like you hear tell. They ain't bad if you don't let them get behind you. Or between you and water. Or catch you too far from the rocks."

"Jings . . .!" sighed both boys, then just sat and stared at the Concho County Comanches.

The opportunity was too much for Eubie Buell.

"Yes, sir, you betcha," he said. "Although like Buck says the Injuns ain't too much, you still got to look sharp, happen they make any funny moves. You get careless, your hair is going to end up on some Kwahadi buck's belt." He bent his head toward the firelight, parting his own long sun-bleached locks.

"You see that there scar? You know who put it there with his war ax? Peta Nacona hisself, that's all. Only the head chief of the whole Comanche nation. The one as was the husband of Cynthia Ann Parker. As was finally kilt by Cap Sul Ross and his Texas Rangers in the big fight on Pease River. Me and the other boys, here, we was helping

Cap Ross that day and believe you me, if we hadn't of been there them Rangers wouldn't have stood a chance. That was December of 1860. You don't believe it, you just ask next time you're down at Ranger headquarters in San Antone."

"Jupiter!" exclaimed the second boy. "I'd surely like to do that but it's a powerful long ways to San Antone."

"Mr. Buell counted on that," put in Willy Bill aridly, adding to Eubie, "You hadn't ought to bore our guests with such self-talk, Eubank. We'd ought to show more interest in their local affairs. Ain't that so, Buck? Like maybeso could these here boys show us around town tonight."

The other Comanches brightened, looking to Buck, and Todo MacLean said quickly, "Yeah, Buck, how about it? We going into town or ain't we?"

"Say," suggested the first of the city boys, before Buck could answer, "you all want to go in and see the sights, why not start with our place? Cousin Airybelle is having a cotillion tonight—that's a fancy dance—and there's folks coming from as far away as Henderson and even Nacogdoches. You'd be more'n welcome."

"Airy Bell," said Eubie softly. "That a feller or a girl?"

"Girl," answered the first boy. "First cousin from over to Tuscumbia, in Alabama. Staying the summer."

"*A girl . . . !*" sighed Eubie reverently, and fell still.

"Is she purty?" asked Todo presently.

"Folks say," nodded Cart, the sober one of the twins. "Don't they, Claibe?"

"Sure," said Claibe. Then, expansively, "I suppose she's pretty, if you like girls."

"I like them," vowed Willy Bill. "This here Airy Bell, she's a sure enough looker?"

"She's a girl," insisted Claibe stubbornly.

"That's the best kind," said Eubie. "I never seen much of a way to improve on a girl."

"Well, Buck," demanded Little Bit Luckett, "we going to the party or ain't we?"

"Why," answered Buck nervously, "we ain't even been asked proper. These two ain't giving the dance, it's their folks, or maybeso their lady cousin."

"That's so," agreed Claibe. "But we was told to ask who we pleased. Weren't we, Cart?"

"If you say," nodded Cart.

"You'll come, then?" said Claibe to Buck, his eagerness genuine.

"Well, maybe," hedged the latter. "What time?"

"Along about nine. Soon as she's good and dark. You'll

hear the music strike up. Going to be five fiddles, a brass
trumpet and a foot drum all the way over from Shreveport.
It won't be like anything you ever heard in Concho County."

"And with a girl, too," murmured Willy Bill. "A real live
girl."

"There'll be lots of them," said Claibe. "A dozen, anyway.
Maybe fifteen or twenty."

"I want to see that Airy Bell," vowed Eubie.

Buck suddenly struck his fist into his palm.

"You'll see her!" he decided, blue eyes alight. Then, more
calmly to the twins, "It's a deal, you all. We'll be there. But
you be sure and tell your folks that you asked us, you hear?"

"Yes, sir, you bet!" promised Claibe. "Our name's Amon.
He's Carter and I'm Claiborne. Father's Dr. Lamar Amon.
Ask anywheres in town for our place."

"She lie on the yonder side?" said Buck.

"Yes, sir. Big white place stuck way back in the loblolly
pines. Six or seven nigger shacks built out behind. You can't
miss it."

"Nigger shacks?" said Buck curiously. "In your back
yard? Whatever for?"

"For our niggers, naturally. What else would they be
for? Don't you know anything about niggers?"

"Not too much," admitted Buck. "We got mainly Injuns
in our part of the country. Them and a few Mexicans.
First darkies we seen was in Fort Worth. They acted mighty
friendly. They give you any trouble? I mean like the Injuns?"

"They do what they're told," answered the town boy a
little quickly. "They're *our* niggers."

"I suppose that's so," said Buck. "I'd forgot." He frowned
a moment, then nodded. "Well, thank you for the invitation to your cousin's party, Claiborne. You, too, Carter.
We will hope to see you there later on."

The twins grinned happily at Buck's politeness, waved
good-bye, started off toward the road. Three steps away,
Claibe stopped and came back.

"Say," he said, "I plumb forgot to ask you boys what
you're doing in these parts. Where you going?"

Buck looked across the fire at him. He stood up, his young
face going serious.

"We're going to the war," he answered quietly.

Claiborne Amon widened his eyes.

"The war?" he finally managed unbelievingly. "You mean
the big war, the one going on between the states?"

"You know a better one going on between anybody else?"
said Eubie Buell belligerently. But Buck said, "Hush, Eubie,

they don't mean to be smart," then answered the city boys earnestly. "Yes, it's the big war we're going to. The one against the Union. We've took our oaths to march to Richmond, in Virginia. We're going to serve with General John Bell Hood and the Texas Brigade when we get there. We mean to fight for the South and for freedom with the last drop of our blood."

Claibe threw up his hands excitedly.

"But you're only boys like Cart and me!" he said. "You can't fight against the North. With all those grown-up soldiers. And real guns? And cavalry swords? And field cannons? Why you might get killed!"

Todo MacLean stiffened. His six feet three inches of prairie bone and muscle looked nine feet tall.

"If you're big enough, you're old enough," he said disdainfully. "That's the rule where we come from."

"Ease off, Todo," ordered Buck. "These here are city boys. They ain't had our chances."

"The hell!" snorted Little Bit, his bantam rooster's ire aroused. "They've had *better* chances than ours, and by twice. They're halfways closer to Richmond than us and they ain't tooken one step to join up!"

Quiet Cart, the shy twin, edged forward to face the Western boy.

"It's just that we never thought to join up," he said in his soft voice. "We're only just sixteen and it never occurred to us that boys our age could go and fight. Nobody ever said anything about it before."

Little Bit, who had no capacity for sustaining anger, put his hand impulsively on the city boy's shoulder.

"Cart," he said, "I'm downright sorry I spoke out."

"I told you all," said Buck, "to keep your mouths shut."

"Yes, well, they're opened now," said Eubie, "and I reckon it's a little late in the afternoon for closing them. I say there's only one decent thing to do to show these East Texas boys we ain't really mean and small. That's to swear them into the Comanches and take them along with us to Richmond."

"You're funning!" gasped Claibe Amon. "You wouldn't actually let us go to the war with you!"

"Equal rank and rights, regulation oath and all," maintained Eubie. "That's my vote."

"Buck's the leader," broke in Miller Nalls. "It'd be for him to say."

Buck, cornered, studied the city boys carefully.

"Would you want to go with us?" he asked them thoughtfully. "It's powerful hard doings living off the land. It would be like nothing you ever done and you might not make it through. You'd best think about it some."

The Mendota boys looked at Buck Burnet standing there in the jump and flicker of the firelight. The picture of him —wide hat, low gunbelt, high boots, big Sonora spurs— was simply too rich for city-starved imaginations. Claiborne Amon closed his eyes, still not able to accept such wild luck.

"You would never do it," he repeated. "You'd never really swear us into your troop and let us go along."

"In the Comanches," said Buck, "we do things by company vote. If you say you want to come with us, we'll take a count of hands right now."

"Cart?" said Claibe, turning to his brother.

Cart shook his head.

"Boys," he told the Comanches, "I would be prouder to go with you than with General Hood himself."

Slow-moving Miller Nalls stepped to the quiet twin, put a thick arm around his shoulder. "All right," he said, "now you got two votes. What you say, Buck?"

Buck looked around at the rest of the Comanches.

One by one the hands came up, even J.C. Sutton's.

"You can take the oath before we march in the morning," Buck said. "Meanwhile check with your folks for permission, get your outfits together and say your good-byes. You got good horses?"

"We haven't got any horses," Claibe admitted uneasily. "Not of our own."

"We'll get them," said Cart quietly. "We'll take Father's Morgans."

"The carriage bays?" said Claibe. "You're daft, Cart. Father would skin us alive."

"We'll take the Morgans," said Cart. "We don't have to steal them. We can pay for them with the inheritance money we got from Grandma Amon. We'll leave it on Father's desk."

"I don't know, I don't know," worried Claibe. "He gave a scad for those Morgans—brought them all the way from Louisville. He'd have the sheriff . . ."

"You got to have good horses," Buck interrupted. "Poor stock won't stay with these Concho ponies."

"I don't know," Claibe began again, but his brother said quietly, "What time you want us here in the morning, Buck?" and Buck replied, "First light; can you make it?"

Claibe wagged his head as though to say he didn't see how they could, but once more Cart answered quickly, "We can make it, Buck. I'd rather be a Concho County Comanche than president of the Confederate Army."

"Armies don't have no presidents," announced Little Bit. "They got generals."

"Never mind what armies got," said Eubie. "We got a dance party to get ready for. What you say, boys?"

The Comanches responded with a kiyiying round of coyote yips and Eubie yelled, "Watch out for us, you hear, Claiborne? We'll be there with bells on!"

Claibe, restored in command for the Amon side, grinned and called back, "Sure thing. You Concho boys will put more life in Airybelle's musicale than any affair since the Davy Crockett Ball at Nacogdoches."

"Airy Bell!" sighed Eubie Buell. "What a name!"

"Yes," murmured Todo MacLean worshipfully. "I will bet she is beautifuller than a queen. Airy Bell, Airy Bell. Ain't it got a grand ring to it, though?"

"More lovelier," said Eubie, "than anything I have heard in my whole life. I'm in love, boys. I tell you my heart's plumb gone. I am shook to my shoes. Airy Bell, Airy Bell, Airy Bell . . ."

"Your heart," said Little Bit dourly, "ain't all that's plumb gone, Eubank."

"Coming from you, I take that as unsalerated praise," Eubie conceded with a bow. "Many, many thanks."

"All right," Buck said, "let's get ourselves cleaned up. And when we get there let's mind our manners and act like what we are—the Concho County Comanches."

5 The Nonmilitary Ball

IT WAS NEARING nine o'clock, the moon climbing low over the Sabine, when the Comanches, long hair slicked with antelope tallow, boots dressed with bear oil, young beards shaved clean and necks and ears scrubbed to a creekwater shine, set out for town.

Riding through the town they were confounded to see frame houses made of sawmill lumber, some of them two and even three stories high, set among pruned elms, chinaberries and pecans, their green lawns trimmed neat as a clipped sheep's back. And wood or crushed rock sidewalks

everywhere, and even raised crossings of paved brick at
the street corners for going over in wet weather! The
clincher came, though, with the oil lamps lining the town
square four ways around. To see those blue lights burning
atop the black iron poles, not fluttering one breath behind
their glass faceplates, was purely astonishing. And a little
frightening.

When they found the twins' home they were not ready
for what it represented either.

To begin with it wasn't the Amon "place" but the Amon
plantation, a fact verified by the Comanches when native
caution led them to tie their mustangs in a hedgerow and
circle the mansion before announcing themselves. What
Claibe had described as half a dozen nigger shacks now
loomed in the moonlight as four rows of three big dogtrot
slave cabins, accommodation enough for fifty or sixty grown
people. And most of those fifty or sixty seemed presently
at work in the rear yard of the main house readying the
food and drink for the cotillion. Buck and the boys were
staggered. The cookhouse alone was bigger than any building they had seen in West Texas. The open-front barbecue
pavilion was long enough to hold a full Comanche council
meeting, the springhouse bigger than the Paint Rock Hotel,
the carriage barn, according to Eubie Buell's awed whisper,
"huger than the Ranger barracks in San Antone!"

As the intimidated trespassers lay up in their cover of
lilac and spiraea bushes at lawn's edge, Little Bit nudged Buck
and muttered, "Say, ain't that Cart standing yonder in the
drive?" Buck looked and said, "Yes, that's Cart."

"Cart don't talk so much as the other one," said Miller
Nalls, "but I cotton to him more. I think we'd ought to
one of us sneak over there and leave him know we're here."

"That's so," said Eubie. "It would be a heap politer than
laying here spying on him."

"You go, Eubie," Buck directed. "You're the best sneak
we got."

"Excepting for you, maybe," answered the other boy.
"Next to you, Buck, owl feathers and milkweed fuzz ain't
in it. You could outstalk a housecat wearing goosedown shoes.
However, I'll have a stab at it."

He was back shortly with Carter Amon. When one of
the ranch boys asked him about the great number of colored
people his reply was prompt and firm.

To begin with, he said, the people were just as content
and happy as they seemed. They had more fun out of their

work than most white folks. Cart claimed his father would not tolerate an "ugly" nigger about the place. He would not have one on Amon plantation longer than it took to ship him down the river to the market at Baton Rouge. So the Amon niggers were all good niggers.

"They do look mighty well fed," agreed Todo MacLean.

It was a fact, too, Carter Amon said, that their colored people were better off than half the brush-hut white trash in East Texas. They didn't know what it was to have one of their people run off at Amon plantation and Cart had never seen a Negro whipped on their place. It was lies, black and dark, they printed in the Northern papers about slavery in the South, he concluded.

Buck said he had never seen a Northern newspaper and wouldn't know the Yankee views on keeping colored people penned up. Except, of course, that everybody knew there weren't any slaves held up North.

About this time Eubie broke in to return the talk to much more interesting subjects.

"What the hell," he wanted to know, "about that there dance party and them creamy girls up yonder? Ain't that fiddle music I hear ascraping?"

All the boys cocked their heads anxiously and Willy Bill jumped up and cried out, "Come on, or we'll miss her clean!" But even as they set out to be presented in the receiving line to Dr. and Mrs. Amon, they heard the lovely strains of the first waltz floating through the open casements of the ballroom. The measured notes sobered them.

"Buck," pleaded Miller Nalls, "let's hold up a bit and watch through the windows. I ain't got the bareface gall to bust in there, cold turkey. Not amongst all them town folks in their white suits and fluffy dresses. I got to sort of lay back and build up to it, gentle."

"Me, too," admitted Buck, adding to the others, "come on, we'll scout it a little closer like Miller says."

At once some audible resentment arose and Buck stiffened. He knew what Eubie, Willy Bill and the lot of them —J.C. Sutton for sure—were thinking. It was that he, Buck, didn't have the common gumption to go through with his own commands; in this case the nerve to brace up and march around to those high doors out front, yes, and straight on through them, smack into that flossy ballroom. And the shameful truth was he didn't have that nerve. He would rather have taken a horse-whipping than face the glitter from the glass chandeliers and wall-bracket candelabras blaz-

ing away in there. It was too much to think of all those city
folks, so breedy and well brought up, standing there staring at
him and his roughly clad boys from Concho River.

Yet he was still Buck Burnet and still the leader.

"All right," he said, "we will go in by the front doors.
See that you mind your manners with those girls. No
catamounting, no jumping up, no heel-clacking, no fandango
yelling or Mexican yelping. You all hear me?"

The Comanches acknowledged that they did by stream-
ing off after Cart Amon, halfway through his speech, leaving Buck to finish up talking to himself and Miller Nalls.

"Buck," groaned Miller, "I cain't face up to it!"

"Miller," answered Buck, jaw set like Concho caprock,
"you got to face up to it. *Forward march . . .!*"

The only merciful thing about the appearance of the
Comanches at the Amon cotillion was its brevity. When
the white-gloved Negro doorman flung wide the carved
panels and announced, as proudly instructed to do by young
Master Cart, "Captain William Buckley Burnet and the gentlemen of his command from Concho County," Cart's mother
put her hand to her temple and swooned into the arms of his
father. Dr. Amon, surrendering his wife's form to a house
servant, bellowed at his two heirs to see him at once in
their rooms. The last Buck saw or heard of the twins was as
they retreated ahead of their father up the spiraling stair-
case, with Cart stoutly maintaining the ranch boys were
personal friends of his and, moreover, patriots on their way
to enlist with General Hood and the Texas Brigade to fight
in the war for Southern independence. This loyalty was
terminated by what sounded like a very solid whack of
caning hickory, accompanied by a muffled, wounded bleating,
and Buck wisely called out the order to fall back and regroup.

The affair was prevented from becoming a rout solely
by the appearance on the veranda of Miss Ariadne Lassiter
of Tuscumbia, Alabama, to plead that some people in Texas
still did not understand about the war. Sacrifice at home
made it nowhere near as popular as it had been six months
ago. A few scalywags were even beginning to mutter out loud
that Houston had been right, which meant, of course, that
Texas should have declared for the Union. It was different
in Alabama, cried the trembling girl; and it was as an
Alabama girl, she said, that she now begged them to come
back into the ballroom and be received like the brave soldiers
of the Confederacy which they were on their way to becoming.

Offhand delivery and lovely source considered, it was a stirring speech. But Buck and the boys, having been once bitten by East Texas patriotism, were now twice shy of it. They could not face the prospect of reëntry.

"Ma'am," Buck said, "we are all mightily beholden to you and most grateful for your courtesy and kindness. But for you we would have gone away thinking wrong of the war. As it is, we see that it ain't lost yet and, indeed, never can be with grand ladies like yourself to stand by and urge on our boys. We started out from home with only God's help but now we have yours. It will mean a great deal to us, ma'am, in the troublesome times to come."

From what secret well of dignity Buck had drawn his reply he could not have stated.

"May the dear Lord bless and keep you, every one," Miss Lassiter murmured, lavender eyes aglow. Then, graciously extending her perfumed hand toward Buck and lowering her thick lashes in a way which sent a shiver of pure panic speeding through him, she whispered, "Farewell, Captain Burnet . . . !"

Desperately Buck looked to the Comanches for help. Into the breach stepped handsome J.C. Sutton. Bending low over Ariadne's hand, he took it in his own and kissed it with as gallant a flourish as any plantation dandy from Mobile to Montgomery.

What the Menard County boy whispered to the Alabama girl did not reach the straining ears of his fellow Comanches. But they did not need the words, only the example. One by one, clumsy about it as any frontier boys would be, yet in their lean, dusty-booted ways, compellingly graceful, too, they followed J.C. in kissing the hand of Miss Ariadne Lassiter of Tuscumbia, Alabama.

They knew they had come upon something for which they had no definition and no defense. And that had it not been for a gracious and lovely Alabama girl they would not have been able to march on with their heads nearly so high, nor their hearts halfway so determined, as they would still be able to do despite the trouble at Amon plantation.

6 First Decision

UNDER THE CIRCUMSTANCES none of the Comanches expected the Amon twins to show up the following morning. Hence, when Buck rolled them out at 5:00 A.M. and passed the order to "rise and shine," they were astonished to see the blond boys coming down the Mendota road astride two blooded bays. Carter and Claiborne Amon were accordingly taken in, swearing on Miller's Bible to obey all commands and stay with the troop until death or injury might part them from it. Claibe took his oath light-heartedly but Cart spoke his promise as though he were giving it to John Bell Hood in front of the entire Texas Brigade.

Watching the ceremony, Eubie said to Willy Bill curiously, "Which one you think will stick it the best?"

"The little one," replied Willy Bill without hesitation. "Even though he ain't got the bone and muscle for blowing his nose. He's dead sober like old Miller and them's the kind that sticks."

"That's so," said Eubie. "The big one's too quick to flash his teeth and talk up. I never did trust a kid with too much grin. They seldom got the grit to go with it."

"Hush up that talk in the ranks," ordered Buck.

"Yes sir," said Eubie. "Now like—"

"Eubie," scowled Buck, "slack off."

"I hear you, General," answered Eubie, throwing Buck an overdone salute. "I'm slacked."

"General?" said Cart Amon, puzzled. "I thought you were a captain, Buck."

"Cart," said Buck, "I ain't nothing. The boys just voted me leader to Richmond. We ain't none of us soldiers so far."

They left it at that, setting out along a back road wide of town. The Amons didn't care to have the neighbors seeing them off on their father's Morgan coachers despite having left him a signed paper taking the team's value out of their inheritance money.

On the third afternoon as they neared Marshall, the sun, which had not failed them a daylight minute the past week, turned a peculiar pale bronze. The boys drew in and bunched their mounts behind Buck, their eyes following his, first north, then south, then east and west. They saw nothing. They waited, listening intently.

It grew so still they could hear Grandpa Luckett's watch inside Little Bit's horsehide vest. Even the mustangs strained to catch a vagrant sound.

Twenty seconds later they heard it, faint, far away, keening eerily to itself like a crazy person. Then it began to hum like a million hiving bees, although the wind did not move a mane hair on the crouching mustangs nor stir a grass blade on the surrounding prairie.

"Twister," said Buck, low-voiced.

The others, reared since infancy with the dread of the sound, did not argue the forecast.

"It's the time of year," led off Miller Nalls matter-of-factly.

"Show me a six-foot cutbank," said Little Bit, getting to cases.

"I'll settle for a bull wallow," offered Eubie.

"Me," announced Willy Bill, of the bear-dog bravery, "make mine a seven-foot posthole chambered to take a set of twenty-two caliber hips and forty-four Winchester shoulders."

"Yes," added J.C., mean-eyed, "and reamed-out sixty caliber Sharps at the top to let in your big mouth."

"Never you mind my big mouth," said Willy Bill. "Just don't get in my way when I start to dig."

J.C. shook off the other's friendly tone.

"You had better take a tuck in that grin of yours," he said, "or I'll straighten it out permanent for you."

"All right," he said, trying to make it sound steady and calm, "let's leave off the horsing around."

"Who's horsing around?" asked J.C. flatly.

"Nobody," Buck shrugged. "Come on, J.C., we're all on the same side. Let's simmer down and get going."

"Which way you meaning to go?" demanded J.C.

Buck toughened and stared him down. After a moment he kneed his steeldust to one side so that any fire of J.C.'s would not endanger the other Comanches. Then he said to him very quietly, "We're going my way, J.C.," and sat waiting for him to make his play.

While this exchange went on, Miller Nalls was drifting his mount around behind J.C. Now he eased his Springfield carbine from its underleg boot and came up on the trouble-maker's blind flank, as the latter swung his mount to face Buck's.

"You kiss my foot," he said to Buck, "and the same for

the rest of you volunteer heroes. Me, I'll cut my stick to suit myself."

"Not today you won't," Buck told him.

"Today or any other day," gritted J.C., clawing his gun hand.

"No need to push it, man," said Buck soothingly. "We all threw in to go to Richmond in a bunch. We give our words and hands on it. Where's your argument to that?"

He had caught Miller's play and was stalling to permit him to take J.C. But J.C. was not waiting.

"Fill your hand, damn you!" he yelled at Buck.

"Now, J.C.," Buck said, "you know I ain't got no chance drawing against you."

"By God, you had better take a chance," cried the other. "So help me Christ I'll cut you down anyways."

They could all see his jaw muscles snake and his eyes go bad. It was then Buck said level-voiced to Miller Nalls, "All right, take him, Miller."

Miller grunted and brought the Springfield down across J.C.'s forearm. The crack of it sounded as though the bone had split from wrist to elbow. J.C. yelled and grabbed his arm. The paint pony spooked out from under him, dumping him in the trail. For the second time in seven days J.C. Sutton was knocked unconscious and for the second time picked up and put across his saddle by Little Bit Luckett and Todo MacLean.

Buck called above the building moan of the tornado, "Better lace him on tight this trip. Wrists to boots under the belly. This is going to be a cinch-buster."

"And a fencepost puller and a privy mover and a county-seat shifter and a few other things," added Todo.

Buck frowned and shook his reins.

"Get aboard your ponies," he ordered Little Bit and Todo. "Rest of you look sharp. Everybody rope themselves together back of me, single file. You Amon boys space out. Cart behind me, Claibe behind Miller. You others string out back of Claibe. Let's go; we're going to have to rump up to this blow and drift with her. Hop it . . .!"

There was the usual flurry of four-letter comment by way of belittling anything that smacked of orders, but even Eubie Buell was beginning to consider the weather seriously.

The sky, north, west and south, was the color of an old Comanche tipi skin, dirty brown and sooted with the grease and smell of a thousand cookfires. Six hundred yards away they could see the funneling out of the cyclone. They could see, too, the wall of blackness for which the funnel was the foreguard. Only to the east, toward Marshall, was there clear sky remaining.

In that direction lay their chance of escape. It was not much of a target, and their hopes of hitting it were, in Eubie's subdued estimate, "about two times double ought divided by zero." Yet there was one thing Eubie and all the others were certain of: if there was any chance whatever of their getting to safety, Buck Burnet was the one who could do the getting.

The latter understood this confidence. As the last rope was tied and he started out with the Comanches strung in line behind him, the weight of their trust bore down upon him fearfully. He glanced around at white-faced Cart Amon and waved him a grinning salute. He was rewarded by a shakily returned grin and salute. The following instant, however, the beacon light of clear sky ahead was snuffed out and the midnight hell of wind was screaming down his throat crushing his breath back into his lungs.

It came to him powerfully there in the yammering blackness that he should have let them go their own ways as J.C. had wanted. And he should never have allowed the Amon twins to join up in Mendota. Had he not been so stubborn he would now have only himself to worry about. As it was, eight lives were on his conscience and in his care. If he blundered one step, rode over a single arroyo edge, let the rope behind him get cut, or fouled and broken, if he even failed to keep a tight line every solitary minute, one or more of those poor boys—but the hell with that! He was still Buck Burnet and he was still not afraid of anything but God and a good woman.

He fought to get back his stolen breath. Gasping, he forced the strength of it into him once more, drove the steeldust forward with a smothered shout of defiance. It was no good. No damned good at all. Fear was in him to his finger tips, and deadly doubt. The wind screamed at him, clutching his throat, shutting off his air again. He gagged, retched, was sick and could breathe once more. He bit at the thick air, gulped it down, held it there, struggled on. The world was blind and he was blind with it. He could not see his horse's ears or his own hands holding the reins.

If this was the result, the reward, the meaning of leadership, Buck did not want its responsibilities ever again. He wanted only to live, to keep breathing, to come once more into God's fresh air and clean sunshine, and to do it all by himself with no one else to have to share it with when he got

there. If with God's help he could do that, could win free
of this howling inferno, then both the war and his Concho
County Comanches could go to hell.

Buck Burnet had a far better place to head for. Home.

7 Route March

BUT BUCK DID NOT GO HOME. He was a Burnet. On into
the raging blindness he led the way. He held a course as
nearly as any human being could guess, toward Marshall
and away from the whirling center of the wind. Seconds
were like minutes, minutes like entire days. Nothing had
any meaning except the funneling roar of sound which
surrounded him. Yet Buck would not quit.

Buck's first hint of safety came with Eubie Buell's cheerful rendering of a ribald Concho County ballad concerning
the Texas weather. Since he could plainly distinguish each
four-letter word of the song, he knew the core of the great
wind had gone by and that they had only to slog out the
misery of rain and mud which would follow it to be safe
in Marshall by nightfall.

The rain came after the wind as he had guessed, but it
was more than merely miserable. It was a cloudburst of
tropic proportions. Buck ordered the *reatas* left in place,
drove the steeldust forward once more. It was like fording
a river underwater. The rain fell as though it were never
going to get the chance to come down again. Within the
first quarter-hour sheet water lay on the open prairie to the
horses' fetlocks. Buck cursed and slowed up.

It was frightening. Of natural light there was not enough
to see half a pony's length. Still Buck knew they must not
stop. The streams in that part of the country drained toward
the Gulf, slanting across the path to Marshall. If they got
down to wait for daylight, the rain continuing the way it
was, they would wake up with every creek on the prairie
running forty feet wide and fifteen miles an hour. The real
rivers such as the Sabine ahead and the Trinity behind
would be so wide a pistol shot would not carry them and
a swum horse would wash downstream a hundred and fifty
yards a minute. The answer was that they had to push on,
trusting to luck to get them across all the serious water be-

tween them and Marshall before the big rise from up-country hit the midlands. The course was obvious to Buck but he held up and took a vote on it nonetheless.

Five of his own boys backed him solidly but the Amon twins were split, Claibe voicing loud fears, Cart seeming to hint at the same feelings through his hesitancy, while J.C. could not utter a word one way or the other.

When the storm broke and the stars came out it was twenty minutes past 4:00 A.M. and they were standing on the edge of a piece of water which rain had never put there and which spread away from them in all visible directions save the one from which they had come. Half an hour later when the stars had paled and the real daylight gained, they could make out where they were and how close they had come to certain disaster.

Before them and upon both sides stretched an awesome sheet of smoking brown water, bordered by a nightmare mat of sawgrass, cattail rushes, drowned cottonwoods, cypress knees, drift limbs and contorted snags. The keenest eye among them could see no end to the open water which began beyond this primordial jungle fringe and of them all only Buck realized where they must be. That was the great Caddo Lake Swamp out there!

When he realized this, and realized, too, how near he had come to leading his faithful troop into the poisonous waters in last night's rain and darkness, he grew shakenly humble. Any intelligent person in Texas knew that more poor innocent folks had disappeared into this fearsome swampland than had been scalped by all the Indians or siphoned off by all the twisters that ever raised a war whoop or a barn roof in the entire Lone Star State. It was time to look up to that clean blue sky yonder and say a few deep-felt words of thanks.

8 Beyond the Call

PRAYERS PROVED NO BETTER than blind luck.

The rain had made a hock-deep quagmire of the terrain around Caddo Lake. Trouble fell upon them in the rank sawgrass clearing of their first night's camp. They had struggled all day through swampy brush south of the lake. Early in the march the city boys had begun to fade. Claibe had been first, complaining of the mud and catclaw thorn, threatening vaguely to quit and turn back. Still he had kept up with the others, not asking any particular favors except that of talking too much. Cart, the quiet one, had not spoken at all, yet he was plainly giving out. His color was ashen, his hands had a weak tremble in them. By late afternoon he was slumped in the saddle. Just before twilight, when he would have fallen but for the help of Miller Nalls who had been mothering him since noon, Eubie and Willy Bill, riding next in line, saw tears running down Cart's cheeks. If Miller saw them, he gave no notice. He did call a halt of the day's ride, however. With the skill of their frontier knowledge, the men got a supper fire going.

After the meal Cart called across the fire to Buck, asking if he might talk with him alone. Claibe at once took alarm.

"Wait a minute," he said. "What's the matter that your own brother can't hear? What's up anyhow?"

Cart turned on him, white-faced.

"You stay out of it," he told him. "My business is with Buck."

Claibe got up and left the fire with the others.

"Buck," the Mendota boy said when they were alone, "I can't go on with you. There's something wrong with my leg."

"Yes," said Buck, "I've been watching you. You ain't moved a foot since we lit down."

"I can't," answered the city boy. "Something hit me in the knee during that high wind. It felt like a cannonball, Buck. Nearly knocked my horse over."

"Likely a rock," Buck said. "They fly like sand in a twister." He squinted at the stiffened leg. "Is it mashed bad, you think?"

"I don't know. I haven't looked at it."

"You ain't, Cart?"

"No, sir. My pants' leg is stuck tight to it. I couldn't manage to look without making trouble. You know, having the others stop to ask what's wrong, and like that. I surely don't want to make you any trouble, Buck, nor them either."

"You figure it's any trouble for us to stop and help you, Cart?"

"I figure the big thing is to get on, Buck. Like you said, we got to get to Richmond in time."

"Well you done real good, Cart, but next time you yell out when you're hit. It's my job to take care of my men." He picked a brand from the fire. "Let's have a look at that 'cannonshot' of yours. You may get first honors for being wounded in battle."

"Sure," said Cart, trying to grin through gritted teeth. "Go easy, though, Buck, I'm not tough to it yet like you Concho boys."

Buck nodded and slit the lower trouser leg with his knife. The cloth still stuck to Cart's knee and when he put force on it to free it, the city boy groaned and went limp. Buck, looking at his color, tried moving the injured leg. The knee was locked tight. He winced, calling low-voiced to Miller and the boys.

"Give me a hand here. Cart's passed out. He's been riding since last night with a bad-broke leg."

Moments later, when they had soaked the blood- and serum-plastered cloth from Cart's leg and were gazing at the white-bone pulp of the shattered knee, Buck looked up at the Comanches and said, "You know what he told me? He told me he wasn't tough to it yet like us Concho boys. . . ."

Cart did not sleep until nearly dawn, but at last exhaustion claimed him. His fever rose with the sun, however, and he began talking wildly. By the time it was broad day and the coffee boiled, Buck had reached his decision—Carter Amon had to have medical help.

Buck remembered a Mexican rider who had worked for his grandfather getting a leg bone broken out through the flesh in a bad horse fall. When they had not been able to get him to the doctor in Lampasas due to high water across the roads, gangrene had set in and the man was dead within two days. On the third morning the creeks had dropped and they had taken the body on into town to bury it legally. Buck could still hear the doctor telling his grandfather how they could almost certainly have saved the man's life had they reached Lampasas in time, but that once gangrene got up a leg beyond the point of amputation there was nothing any doctor could do.

Buck tried to shake off the memory. Cart was going to be all right. They would get him to town in time. The first thing in that direction was to find people in this lowland *brasada,* this swamp-basin brush jungle, people who would know the way to the nearest settlement and doctor.

"Miller," said Buck, rising, "tell the boys to saddle up. We're pushing on. I want every man except you and Claibe fanned out front scouting for cabin smoke. You got that?"

"Yes, sir," answered Miller, and turned to repeat the order to the Comanches, who were already tightening their cinches.

Quickly the troop spread out, working south. Miller and

Claibe followed, siding Cart Amon. Buck rode between parties, maintaining contact. It was nearing dusk when the first report came in.

"Ho, Buck!" cried Eubie Buell, waving from a slight rise to the right. "Over here—smoke ahead!"

Buck acknowledged the call and fired three signal shots to bring in the others. Together the troop swung east to follow Eubie. Cart Amon was now unconscious, carried like a child by Miller Nalls. Claibe Amon, crying openly, rode behind Miller leading Cart's horse. Buck brought up the rear.

Ahead Eubie had found the dwelling heralded by the rising smoke. But when Buck and the boys saw it, their hearts dropped. It was not a house but a *jacal,* a brush hut of the type put up by Mexican squatters or by maverickers working the thicket for cowhides to sell to the tallow works at Brazoria on the Gulf.

"Hold up, here," Buck said. "I'll ride on in."

He put the steeldust on a slow walk toward the *jacal,* moving to within thirty feet of its door before the Big Fifty Sharps boomed and the huge buffalo slug came whistling over his left shoulder.

"Basta, señor!" The voice was high, the accent border Spanish. "That is far enough. You will please to state your business in this place."

"And you, you little bastard," said Buck easily, squinting at the octagon barrel of the big Sharps protruding from the partly opened door, "will please to put down that damned bullgun and come out where I can see you. Elsewise, I will step off this pony and tan the back of your hide dark enough to match the front."

The youngster's appreciation of being called "a man" by a red-headed *Tejano,* who was at least as tall as the eaves of his father's *jacal,* was both instant and encouraging.

"Señor," he said, "a thousand pardons. You are welcome in this house." He stepped out, setting down the rifle as directed. "I am Pablo Massanet—Paul in English."

"Massanet?" repeated Buck. "That's a French name, ain't it?"

"Cajun," said the boy. "My father is Cajun. From Pontchartrain, down the big river, *señor*. His name, too, is Paul Massanet." Noting Buck's continuing puzzlement, he added with a shrug, "It is the mother whose tongue we speak. She is *Mejicana."*

Buck's face lightened.

"I thought you looked Mexican," he said.

"I am many things, as you can see," replied the boy, and

Buck, observing his very dark skin, regular features, peculiarly green eyes and long auburn hair, had to agree. He was an odd mixture all right; white French, brown Mexican and, to judge from the slant of his high cheekbones, red Indian as well.

"I like the Mexicans," he said. "They're fine people."

"I am not Mexican," the boy told him quietly. "I am American."

"By golly, that's right!" Buck smiled politely. "A man takes his daddy's nationality, don't he?"

"Thank you," said the boy. Then, carefully, "Call me Pablo, even though I am American. *Por favor.*"

"*Por supuesto.*" Buck smiled. "Now listen, American . . ."

He quickly told the boy why they had come to the clearing, and asked him if there were any doctors nearby.

"In Marshall only," was his answer. "Three days away by burro cart."

"How many days by horse?" asked Buck.

"*Señor,*" replied the boy, looking past him to the waiting Comanches at clearing's edge, "I can see from here that your friend is too sick to ride a horse. He will go to Marshall in our burro cart, or he will not go at all."

"In three days," said Buck softly, "he may not care which way he goes."

"Bring him in the house," suggested Pablo. "When Big Paul comes home tonight, he will tell us what do do."

Buck thought a moment, tempted. The opportunity for adult advice was strong bait. In the end, too strong.

"Thank you, Pablo," he said, and turned and waved the Comanches to bring Cart on in. Miller and Todo MacLean carried the moaning Amon twin inside and put him upon a clean pallet which Pablo pointed out. As Miller straightened he caught Buck's eye. Buck followed him outside.

Miller said, "Buck, I got the creeps. That poor boy ain't going to make it through the night. He's hot-skinned as a rode-out horse and that leg of his stinks something fierce."

"I know," muttered Buck. "I got a look at it in the lamplight when you brought him in."

"It's all prouded up," said Miller, rolling his eyes. "Weepy-looking around the edges, and puffed like a snakebit hock. Buck, I'm spooked."

"I know, Miller," said Buck. "So am I."

His shoulders sagged.

"Miller, he's got the gangrene. If the leg don't come off, he's going to die."

9 Brief Soldier

IT WAS VERY QUIET in the clearing. Only the harsh breathing of Cart Amon obtruded on the night sounds of the brushland. Buck and Pablo Massanet sat outside against the front wall of the *jacal* watching the moon rise and waiting for Pablo's parents to return. Inside, the Comanches were taking turns putting cold-water rags on Cart's face and body. Presently Buck could stand the silence no longer.

"It's been near four hours," he said to Pablo. "Your folks usually this late?"

"Who can say?" shrugged the other. "Sometimes they stay half a week."

"But you expected them back tonight?"

"Yes."

Again the stillness settled in. But Buck was lonely and worried. Then Pablo asked thoughtfully, "Where is it that you and your friends go? You have a purpose, you are not just wandering. A man can tell."

"Yes," said Buck, "we have a purpose. We are going to fight the war, to fight for our country, for the South."

"Against the North?"

"Sure against the North."

The boy nodded soberly. "Big Paul and I, we have discussed it many times since the war began," he said. "We could never decide which way an American should pledge himself."

"Why," said Buck, "coming to that, it's easy. There's but one way for a Texan to decide and that's for the South." He held up, a tone of suspicion shading his voice. "Say, is that why your father ain't in it? He's agin the South?"

"Oh, never!" protested Pablo. "My father fought with the Rangers of Captain Walker in the Mexican War. He has a decoration from General Scott himself. That was for the arm he lost at Buena Vista. No, it was at Cerro Gordo that he lost the arm. It was the stiff leg and the ribbon from General Taylor that he got at Buena Vista. No matter, you will recognize that my father fought as a true *Tejano*, one loyal to his country. But he is very old, having been forty-seven years at the time of that other war. Now, with but one arm

30

and a leg which will not bend, you must see that he cannot fight in the new war."

"Whew," said Buck, "you can talk enough when you get started, can't you?"

"A man likes to talk when he is understood and when it is important that someone understands him."

"Meaning me, Pablo?"

"But of course, Señor Buck. You must not think a Massanet would not fight for his country."

"Oh, I'd never think that. Not of *your* father, *hombre*. You got any older brothers?"

"No, I have only one sister. And even she ran away four years ago. She was but fourteen years, yet very unhappy. She wanted to see more people, to live more of life, she said. Then she was gone."

"That's very sad."

"Yes, very sad."

The silence returned, grew long. Inside the *jacal* Cart had grown quiet. Too quiet. Pablo stirred.

"Señor Buck. We have talked a long time and have said nothing. Sometimes men will talk in this fashion when they do not wish to hear something which must be heard."

"You have lost me, Pablo. You will have to back up."

"Your friend is still in the *jacal*," said the small boy. "We have not talked him away."

Buck peered at him, his wonder growing at this little weasel's sharp mind.

"You mean the leg, don't you?" he said.

His companion lifted his shaggy head, sniffing the night air like a wild thing.

"Yes," he said. "One can smell it. It smells very sick. The boy will die."

"Unless God won't let him," answered Buck.

"Or you, perhaps, *señor?*"

"Me?" said Buck. "What you getting at?"

"I heard you talk with your big friend earlier; outside, when you thought no one had followed you." The boy paused, listening as though for some sound from far off. After a moment he turned back to Buck. "It has just come to me that Big Paul and my mother will not arrive tonight," he said. "In the morning, early I think, but not tonight." Then, very quietly, "Can the sick one wait until the morning, Señor Buck?"

Buck shook his head. When he answered it was with great weariness. In all the hours waited and talked away, hoping

the boy's father would return and take the decision from
Buck's heart, and its fearsome work from his hands, he had
known this moment must come, and this question with it.
He had known, too, what his answer must be.

Coming stiffly to his feet he looked down at the *brasada*
boy.

"No," he said, "he can't wait," and turned and stooped
low to go into the darkened *jacal* where he must take off the
leg of Carter Amon.

Claiborne Amon slept fitfully in the fireplace corner of
the *jacal*. His dreams were disordered. Time and again he
struggled upward from their grasp, clutching at consciousness. It was some minutes after midnight when he did awaken.
The scene which met his eyes was not immediately credible.

The *jacal*, lit only by the moon at last memory, was
aglare with light. The source of the illumination was a common coal oil lamp, its rays ingeniously refracted by a com-
bination of cracked shaving mirror and polished frying pan,
both articles held by Pablo Massanet and so directed by
him as literally to blaze the collected rays upon the subject
of concentration. It was that subject which held Claibe frozen
with nightmare fear.

Stretched naked upon the *jacal's* scarred wooden table,
his arms and his good left leg pinioned by ropes passed beneath the table, was his brother Cart. The inflamed right
leg was lying free upon a padding of clean bedsheet. Around
the table stood the Concho County Comanches, only Todo
MacLean missing from their number. At the foot of the
table was Buck Burnet, shirtless, lean belly and drawn face
coursing perspiration. At Buck's right waited Miller Nalls
with a dishpan of steaming water. Behind Miller were Little
Bit and Eubie Buell bearing a woven swampgrass hamper
of torn shirting and laundered feed sacking bandages. At
Buck's left stood J.C. Sutton grasping a hackblade saw of
the type used to cut heavy bone in game or beef carcasses.
J.C's dark eyes were watching Buck Burnet and what was
in Buck Burnet's hand—a Kwahadi skinning knife burn-
ished to a glitter and poised in front of the Concho boy
with a grip of determination which suggested he was about
to plunge it into himself.

But he was not.

"Cart," he said to the boy on the table, "I want you to
remember what I told you. Legs have been took off before
this where there wasn't no doctor to do it. And the people

have lived to laugh about it. But you got to do your part."

Cart's lips moved. His voice was so low that only Buck and J.C., bending forward, heard it.

"I believe what you told me, Buck. I believe that I'm going to make it. It's just that I won't be going on to Richmond with the Comanches that's making me cry. I'm not afraid, I swear it, Buck . . ."

"We know you ain't afraid, Cart. You got more insides than all us Comanches put together, you hear?"

As the boy nodded, J.C. reached down and put his hand on his shoulder.

"Cart," he said, "you're a Comanche whether you go on with us or not. If we was half as tough as you, we would all . . ." He broke off, suddenly conscious of Buck leaning in with him. "Never you mind, kid," he finished. "You'll do to ride most rivers with."

Carter Amon tried to smile but the pain and sickness which was in him would not permit it. Buck grimaced, straightening up.

"All right, Willy Bill," he said, "cinch down on him."

Unbuckling his gunbelt, Willy Bill slid it under Cart's leg. The belt rebuckled, he took a turn in its slack, inserted the barrel of his revolver in this loop and began twisting. The makeshift tourniquet bit deep into the healthy pink flesh of the upper thigh. Cart ground his teeth and would not cry out. Buck waved the knife.

"That's enough. Miller . . ."

Miller Nalls moved in. He hooked his arm around Cart's right ankle, putting the infected leg in a vise formed by his thick forearm and doubled bicep.

"All right, Buck," he said. "I've got him."

Buck nodded.

"Cart?" he asked.

"I'm ready, Buck," breathed the Mendota youth. Then, eyes shut in futile attempt to hold back the tears which no Comanche should show but which a town boy from East Texas could not help, "God bless you, boys, and guard our cause. Good-bye, Buck."

Buck dropped his head to hide his own eyes. "All right, Miller," he said, "hold him. A little higher with the frying pan, Pablo. That's good."

It was only when Cart's wrenching scream burst with the plunge of the Kwahadi blade into his thigh that Claibe Amon came raging across the room. It was then the missing Todo MacLean, posted by Buck for the purpose, stepped from the fireplace shadows behind Claibe. He swept him up by the back of his shirt, swung him around, drove his fist into his jaw with the force of a splitting maul.

"Go ahead, Buck," he said. "Claibe's quiet."

The only sounds then were the bumpings of Buck's body as it moved against the table to get better cutting angles with the knife, the hissing spurt of the great femoral artery, the grating halt of the blade as it struck and hung upon the white thigh bone, Buck's suppressed voice saying to J.C., "Saw fast, he's looking bad," the ripping grind of the hack-blade in response to the order, and the choking, gray-faced gasp of Little Bit Luckett as the sawteeth went in and he could not hold his stomach down.

Carter Amon did not regain consciousness. He died in shock from loss of blood at 4:00 A.M. At five o'clock, day-light, the Massanets creaked into the clearing in the family burro cart. When they learned of the tragedy Paul Massanet said he would take the body to Marshall and see that word was sent to the parents in Mendota. He would wait with the body, he said, until it was claimed.

At this, Claiborne Amon, only now released from the ropes which had held him in restraint following his brother's death, cried out anew. No one would touch or bear that body away save himself, and no one but him would stay with it in Marshall or any place else. Buck, then Miller and the others, tried calming him but to no avail. He would only reply with curses and threats to have the law on the lot of them. He singled out Buck for the brunt of his heart-break, claiming he would swear out a murder warrant against him and return with the Wood County sheriff to see it served, if it was the last act of his life.

Buck would not reply to this outbreak but J.C. Sutton would. Stepping toward the Mendota boy he faced him down with his meanest Menard County drawl.

"You ain't going to do a damned thing but get out of here quick," he told him, "and that's all you're wanting to do. You're all mouth and you ain't fit to ride upwind of your brother's body. You got one thing in mind and that's going home. You're a pure yellow son of a bitch and you ain't fooling nobody but yourself. Now you cut your stick and don't you look back while you're acutting it."

In the wordless silence Claibe Amon stared at the other boy. Then his shoulders sagged and he began to weep un-controllably.

"*Christ,*" said J.C. Sutton, and turned away from him.

The dead boy was lifted into the burro cart by the Comanches. They covered him with a canvas butchering sheet, washed clean. As a last thought the troop pennant, a bandanna-sized Confederate flag, was brought out and pinned on the canvas over Cart's breast. Buck bowed his head and said softly, "God bless a brave soldier boy," and they all took off their hats and stood there in silence until he added, "All right, bring up his horse."

They hung Cart's boots upside down in the stirrups and tied the saddled horse behind the cart. This done, they stood back and snapped to attention while Paul Massanet clucked to his small team and started away. It was not yet 5:30 when the cart, followed by Claibe Amon on the second Morgan, disappeared into the catclaw and jack oak of the Caddo swamplands.

Carter Lamar Amon had been a soldier twelve hours less than six days.

10   The Bivouac

GUIDED SKILLFULLY by Pablo Massanet they reached Turtleneck Crossing of the South Bayou at midday. Upon taking his leave Pablo pleaded ardently for Buck to let him go along. Citing his virtues as a tracker, a forager, a spy and a sneakthief of ability, he was, he said, "a man very familiar with the country over in Louisiana," and one who could be of genuine service to them were he allowed to go even so far as Shreveport.

Buck shook his head.

"It ain't that we don't value your offer," he said. "It's that you need to ask leave of your parents, being underage and all."

"And what if I ask the consent, *señor?*"

"Well," Buck grinned, "if you do and can manage to catch up with us, that's another matter."

"Sure," said Eubie Buell, "that's right, Weasel." All the boys, save Buck, called him that. "We will leave you our forwarding address in Shreveport. If you get there after we've took off, just inquire of the local law. They will have heard of us and will know where we have gone."

It was not too good a joke and the Weasel ignored it disdainfully. With an imperative look he motioned Buck to follow him off a few steps.

"Many thanks, Señor Buck," he said when they were alone. "Now there is the one other matter. A message which my father wished me to give you upon the parting. It was that should you in your journeys meet a fine-looking girl, one with slanted eyes and hair the color of a red sunset with dark clouds beneath it—if you just should, señor, come upon such a girl, would you tell her that she is missed and needed and always that she is loved by those who remember her and pray for her each night?"

"Well," said Buck soberly, "that's quite an order to keep in mind, but I reckon it might be arranged." He patted the boy's head. "If we see your wandering sister we will surely do our best to send her home. Now, adios, amigo. Hasta la vista."

"Yes," answered the boy, "that is right. Until we meet again, señor, as you have said. Adios . . ."

He said it with a strange little bow, turned and was gone. Buck stared after him a minute, then went back to the Comanches. Waving them to mount up, he put his steel-dust on the prance and set out to lead them down to the Turtleneck Crossing of South Bayou. If bad things lay behind, good ones must wait ahead. Across South Bayou was Shreveport. Beyond that, Vicksburg and the war. Forward, Comanches!

His fervor lasted to water's edge.

There the Concho boys found an ancient Negro ferryman bedeviled with rheumatics and full of gin to kill the pain. He was mean and hard to bargain with and they had to pay him three prices to get themselves and their seven mounts carried over. Then, traveling on, they found they still had a second arm of the bayou in front of them and no second ferryman to carry them over. They had to find, and bribe, a thieving pack of local Indians into canoeing them across and swimming their horses on lead-ropes behind them. The two crossings took an inhuman toll of their diminishing funds but with the exception of J.C. Sutton, who maintained his aloof silence, the Comanches fell in cheerfully enough behind Buck and pointed their ponies toward the now beckoning lights of Shreveport.

As for Buck, he was proud of his boys and not a little satisfied with himself. They were out of Texas and still intact. He smiled to himself and straightened in the saddle. "Well begun is half done," he told his steeldust pony, and the little horse blew out through his nostrils and bobbed his head in apparent agreement.

On the outskirts of Shreveport Buck halted to study a pole-fenced meadow to his right. In it there was an abandoned barn. It seemed to have a reasonably sound cypress shingle roof and lay on a slight rise so that it ought to prove dry inside. Around it was decent pasture for the horses. With the rain still threatening, it looked like home to Buck Burnet.

But the other Comanches were not pleased. They had been promised the night in Shreveport and they meant to have it there. The devil with camping out here. They wanted to ride on in.

Buck stood firm.

The other boys argued it back and forth. Presently big Todo glanced around at the rest and said, "I ain't speaking for nobody but the MacLean boy but it appears to me as though the only place for us is yonder hayshed."

"Yup," agreed Willy Bill, flavoring it with a wry grin. "From what Captain Burnet tells us, we will be dogbone lucky to last even that distance. Two votes for the barn."

"Three," said Eubie. "I think I might just make it to the first stall, give a running start."

"Tell you what," offered Little Bit, eyeing the distance. "You put three poker tables between me and it and I will hit the damned door in one jump."

"Quit funning, Little Bit," said Miller Nalls. "We done come a far piece past jumping poker tables. We got some serious thinking to do and like old Buck says we had best get to doing it. Ain't that so, Buck?"

Buck agreed with a nod, then turned unexpectedly on J.C. Sutton.

"What do you say, J.C.?" he asked.

"To what?" answered the other, surprised.

"To us holding up here."

"You mean instead of going on into town for that whistle-wetter you promised?"

"You know what I mean, J.C."

Buck said it flat-voiced and they all saw the Menard County youth flinch.

Yet J.C. only gritted his teeth and looked down at his lame pistol arm in such a way that all of them understood his being temporarily hurt was the sole thing keeping him from killing Buck. That put across, he answered the latter quietly.

"Sure thing, Buck, any way you want it. Only remember one thing. I'm going to get you the same way you got me."

Buck looked at him, puzzled. "How's that?" he asked.

"From your blind side and when you ain't looking," said J.C. "Just the dirty, sneaking, chicken-livered way you give it to me both times back yonder. Now you remember that and you be watching for it."

J.C. was not much of a talker. From the length of his warning his listerners could judge how deeply his humiliations at the hands of Buck and Miller had hurt him. It was a funny thing but it almost made them feel sad for him.

As for Buck, he let him ease down a moment, then replied, "All right, J.C., I'll be watching for it," and turned his steeldust to lead the way across the meadow.

The barn proved in better repair than it appeared from the road. There was plenty of scrap lumber for firewood and a rickety loft holding half a ton of good hay for the horses. The boys got the rain-soaked saddles off their mounts, rubbed them down and fed them, then got out of their own wet clothing down to the buff. That done, they lit a roaring blaze and sat around it drying their long-handled drawers, which all buffalo-grass boys wore well into spring, making sure no late blizzard froze their thin-clad bones on some lonely stretch of *llano*. Then, the drawers drying nicely, they drew straws to see who would get stuck with the cooking. As usual it was big Todo.

Fortunately he was the best cook in the band. As such, the best thing about him was that he never understood how it was he got the short straw nine times out of seven. He supposed that he was just naturally unlucky and let it go at that. In the present case he had shortly got together the last of the previous night's cold boiled pinto beans with the final pod of red Texas chili and clove of Mexican garlic, to fry up a good-bye batch of *frijoles refrescas*. Since there had been no noon halt and only mudwater coffee and cold mush for breakfast, the lack of serious criticism was hardly surprising.

"Miller," Buck said, when the last plate was put down, "tell the boys to look over their horses and report back what they find. I want no guesses and no garnishes. You understand?"

"Yes sir," said Miller. "Boys," he relayed across the fire, "Buck wants you should check your ponies. Keep an eye out for brush cuts, stone bruises, quartercracks, saddle galls, sore mouth, all such ordinary cross-country grief. Be sharp but quick. Buck will talk to you soon as you're done."

There was the predicted grumbling but the move toward the feeding mustangs was obediently begun. Only J.C. Sutton did not join it. He sat where he was, staring hot-eyed at Buck Burnet. The latter refused to play to the call. He kept his own gaze down waiting for the others to return. When they had done so, he spoke without looking at J.C.

"What I want is the facts," he said; "I'll furnish my own fancies. You first, Eubie."

The flippant towhead led off unsmilingly, the others following in grudging turn. None of them liked what he honestly had to say, but there was no way around the truth: their saddlestock was done in.

Ironically, the only sound horse in the string was J.C's spooky paint. J.C. apparently understood this and looked, in fact, as though he were planning to make something of it. Yet when the others had completed their reports he did not get up but only continued to sit scowling into the fire, forcing Buck to move first. The latter came uneasily to his feet.

"It's what I thought," he began. "Our stock is next to played out. Boys, me and Miller will have to ride into town and ask around about conditions ahead. Meantime, any of you feel obligated to complain, talk to J.C., he's captain till I get back."

"Now just a damned minute," J.C. started off, but Buck cut him short.

"You can't handle the job, I'll give it to Miller," he said. "I wasn't aiming to put off on you, J.C."

"You're damned well right you wasn't! And you ain't about to either, by God!"

"That's fine by me, J.C. No offense. Miller . . ."

"Now hold on, goddamit!" J.C. stepped toward Buck, dark eyes snapping. "Go on, you and your mulehead friend hit for town. I'll watch these sugartit suckers for you. It ain't like it was nothing I couldn't take care of with my left hand, nohow. Beat it."

Buck could not hide his pleased grin. Catching it, J.C. misread its meaning. His eyes went bad.

"Buck Burnet," he said deadly soft, "don't you forget what I told you. I still mean to take you."

Buck did not make any counterclaims. He only nodded and said, "I won't forget, J.C.," then turned his back on him and started for his horse, Miller following behind him. There was not a sound from any of the other boys as the

two mounted up and brought their ponies back past the fire.
There was still no talk while they rode out of the barn and
off across the water-logged meadow to the Shreveport road.
It was only when they were gone that Little Bit brightened
and said, "Well, hell, they won't be back till daybreak, let's
turn in." To which Willy Bill replied, "Include me in on them
sentiments. I'm as wore out as the path to the privy in
chokecherry time."

These remarks seeming to constitute company opinion,
Little Bit headed the march to the blanket rolls. Shortly
there were only the rustlings and scurryings of the resident
field mice in the loft above to disturb the old barn's quiet.

11 A Message for
the General

IT WAS NEARING ELEVEN at night when Buck and Miller
returned. They had not spent ten cents but had bought a
lot of information. While Todo stirred the fire, the company gathered about to hear the news. None of them expected it to be good news, yet even so it was rough. For
what Buck had to tell them meant they must get rid of
their horses. To a Concho boy this was like being asked to
put a price on his little brother. And this was but the start.

Buck and Miller had been to three horse and mule buyers. Before that they had talked to the station agent of the
Vicksburg and Shreveport Railroad and the superintendent
of the Southern Stagelines concerning travel conditions ahead.
And before that they had inquired of half a dozen towns-
people as to the way the war was going. The answers they
had got were fearful ones.

The Yankees were threatening from Missouri to Mary-
land. In the East the ironclad gunboat *Monitor* had de-
feated the Confederate *Merrimac*, letting McClellan ashore
with his great army at Fortress Monroe, Virginia. McClellan
was preparing to move up the Peninsula directly upon Richmond. In the West Halleck was menacing all the Mississippi
Valley through his new field commander U.S. Grant, who
had already taken Forts Henry and Donelson to the north
and was closing with forty thousand men upon Pittsburg
Landing, far south along the Tennessee River.

It was obvious, Buck concluded, that this threw a dark
light upon their own plans, as well as upon those of the

dear cause they had journeyed so far to serve. One thing remained clear. Any Texas boy wishing to get into the fight had better hurry. That realization had guided Miller and Buck in their inquiries and now must guide the Comanches in their decision.

The facts for that decision were these: It was a new kind of country past Shreveport, the horse buyers had warned. It was thickly settled, with fences around every patch of grass big enough to bury a dog in. Once into Mississippi and Alabama there would be no more free grazing, no more foraging off the country. Now this was no bluff to get them to sell their horses. Far from it. The folks through the country ahead were good-hearted in the main, and loyal Southerners, too. For the most part they would take kindly to seven boys from Texas who were bound for Virginia to fight. But the war was a year old and there would be plenty of others along the way who would charge them three prices simply because they were seven boys from Texas on their way to Virginia. They had to realize they had left the frontier when they crossed Red River. Ahead lay civilization. As ranch boys from the Concho they didn't stand a chance against it. There was simply no use talking, Buck said somberly, or thinking the buyers were trying to hoodwink them. It was a plain fact that they could not hope to ride horseback to Richmond on the fifty dollars they had remaining.

On the other hand, according to the travel agents, they could put their fifty dollars with the money their horses and saddles would bring and purchase tickets which *would* carry them all the way to Richmond. And fast and first class, too. The stage for the connection with the railroad cars into Vicksburg left Shreveport at 2:30 A.M. If the Comanches followed Buck's advice they would vote to sell their horses and take that stage.

"Eubie," he finished sternly, "lead it off."

The sunny-tempered boy grimaced and looked away. It was a sad thing to be asked to do, to give up the pony you had grown up with and which you knew and trusted better than any human. Eubie swallowed hard. "Me," he said shakily, "I'll sell."

"Me, too," said Willy Bill, next in line.

"And me," nodded Little Bit, flinching as his dun pony recognized the sound of his voice and nickered softly.

"Yeah," was all big Todo MacLean could say when Buck shifted his glance toward him.

"Four of a kind beats me," mumbled Miller Nalls, trying in vain to look tough while he said it. All of them gave

him a nod of credit for the try and moved their eyes to
J.C. Sutton. The dark-haired boy eased to his feet.

"Menard County stands pat," he said. "I got a sound
horse and I ain't selling him."

"How come?" asked Buck quietly.

"I need him in my business. I'm pulling out, Buck."

"You dead set on it, J.C.?"

"As a countersunk screw."

Buck nodded in that fair-warning way he had. J.C. knew
the sign by now and, as Buck stepped away to give himself
swinging room, his lame arm came out of his shirt-front
where he had been holding it for want of a sling. That was
the first time any of them had noticed his holster was empty.
By then there was no need to wonder what had become of
the missing gun. It was in J.C.'s sore right hand.

"Turn around," he said to Buck.

The latter hesitated and Miller Nalls entreated him, "For
God's sake do what he says, Buck, he's wore raw!"

"Turn around," said J.C. flatly, "or I'll blow your belly
out."

"Take care, Buck, he's apt to do it," warned J.C.'s kinsman,
Little Bit Luckett. "Them Suttons don't always think straight."

Buck nodded, began his turn. The instant he did, J.C.
shifted the gun to his good left hand, raised it and slashed
its long barrel across the back of Buck's head. Buck went
washy at the knees, slid forward on his face. J.C., not even
looking down at him, called to Little Bit.

"Flop him over and dig out that fifty dollars."

The other boy looked at him unbelievingly. "By God,
J.C.," he said, "you wouldn't do it!"

"Flop him over, Tobin Earl. I want that money."

By the use of the formal name Little Bit knew J.C. meant
it. He bent down and got the money from Buck's vest pocket.
J.C. took it, put it inside his shirt, and started for his horse
without another word or look for any of them. Somehow,
though, he caught the feeling which followed him louder than
any words, and whirled defiantly.

"I ain't taking no more than what's rightly mine!" he
glared. "Goddamit, I've been drove too far, and I'm leaving.
This here fifty dollars is one-fifth of what Tobin Earl won
in Fort Worth. Not counting 'officers' there's five of us.
So it's only my due share of the company pay, by God, and
I'm taking it!"

They did not answer him save with looks.

His own expression grew wilder. He put a boot toe into
Buck's slack body, flopped it halfway over.

"As for him," he said unsteadily, "damn him and his whole idea of going east to enlist. I'm sick to puking of playing soldier boy to his orders." He paused, licking his lips and looking around a little desperately as he saw not one of the stony young faces softening to his excuses. "Me," he yelled at them, "I'm from Menard County and there ain't nobody tells me what to do! You hear that, you noble bastards?"

They nodded quietly but still said nothing. J.C. backed off, looking at them in a strange way. It was almost as though he did not want to leave, now that he had said good-bye. Later several of the boys agreed they had a feeling that if one of them had said just the right, friendly thing at that moment, J.C. would have calmed down and been truly glad to stay. But they did not say it and were eternally sorry in the end.

As for J.C. the moment was past. He went for his paint now in a way which would have been stopped by nothing short of a bullet. Then, white teeth gleaming in the fire's light, he laughed, and called, *"Adios, soldados!"* Then he spun the paint, cut him with the quirt and put him on the dead, wild run out of the barn, showering sods off across the marshy pasture lot to the Shreveport road.

12 Casualty in the Golden Calf

BUCK'S HEAD HURT. It hurt enough to make a Kwahadi Indian cry. Still, he kept the steeldust on a high, hard lope. He did not want to go after J.C. Underneath his hardshell swagger, J.C. had the right makings. He was just one of those Texas boys who imagined there was an insult in every glance, a challenge in every grin, a fact more his own bad luck than anyone else's. Buck's job was to find him and fetch him back, regardless. Let J.C. get away with deserting the troop and the others might be tempted. There might not be a one of them left by the time they got to the Mississippi at Vicksburg.

Ahead now he could see the lights of Shreveport. From the illumination a man would suppose he was coming to a city the size and quality of New Orleans. Buck knew better, having been here in daylight. As with most towns set midway between farm and frontier this one was seventy-five percent

saloon trade. For every school there would be three bars;
for every church, two bawdy houses. It was the sort of
boom-town balance which made a place appear ten times
its true size by night, the time when the few honest men had
put up their shutters and blown out their lamps and when all
who were left were the merchants of sin, each decking his
bar or parlor with a blaze of lights hoping thus to attract
the largest crowd of night crawlers and, thereby, to grow
rich enough so that he could buy himself a pair of honest
shutters and go early to bed cursing his former competitors
for the thieves, criminals, crooks and procurers which they
plainly were.

There was something wrong with this philosophy, Buck
realized, but whatever it was would have to wait. Right
then he was turning off the Red River road into the glittering main stem of Shreveport, Louisiana, and he was not
looking for the answer to man's immorality to man, but
for a particular piece of spotted horseflesh tied outside one
of the two dozen saloons lining the day-bright street. It
was at a time like this that a person appreciated J.C.'s taste
in saddlestock. Your average Western boy would have been
riding a roan or a dun or a steeldust or a brown or one of
the other mousey mustang colors, and it would have been
an all-night job sorting him from the scores of others just
like him, presently lining Main Street. Not so with J.C.
Sutton. He was from Menard County and picked his ponies
to suit himself. Also, thought Buck gratefully, he picked
them so that a person could practically see them from
Menard County. He gave the steeldust a touch of spur, turning him toward the gaudy saloon on his right. At the curb,
he got down and felt the paint's hide under the stirrup fenders.
He was still wet. Good. Granted J.C. would go to the bar for
a bourbon or two before he sought out a table, it was
probable he had not yet lost the money. Buck went in, squinting to the glare of cigar smoke and coal-oil light. Quickly
enough he saw J.C. And saw that he had already had his
bar drinks and bought into a game. A bad one, too.

At the table with him were three older men and a young
girl. What made Buck know the game was not a straight
one, was the girl. J.C. obviously did not realize she was
playing but Buck could see she was holding the fifth hand
despite the fact she was draping herself over J.C.'s shoulder,
making out to help him play the fourth. Yet he couldn't
blame J.C. That girl! She made Buck sweat simply to look
at her from clear across the room. But that was enough of

that. He was here to pick up a soldier who had gone absent without leave and to persuade him to return with the company funds he had borrowed.

Taking a deep breath and forcing his eyes from the girl, Buck set out for the table. But as he drew near it he noted something about that company money which had not been evident from the door. The fifty dollars were no longer J.C.'s to return. They belonged to anyone now—anyone who might get lucky and draw out on the huge jackpot piled high before the players. J.C. did not have a chip, nor a tip, nor a two-bit piece left in front of him. He had shoved every cent of the fifty dollars into a last-hand shot at cleaning the table and buying himself that high-priced streetwalker he had promised the boys he would.

But the game was fixed. Cold deck zero. And it was up to Buck either to unfreeze it, or let it close solid about J.C. and the company money. Under pressure of the unfamiliar role, Buck blundered. Instead of backing off and letting the fifty go, figuring to salvage J.C. and call it a lucky night at that, he set his jaw and moved in.

Stopping at Sutton's elbow he spoke to him in a voice which came out much louder than he had intended.

"J.C., this game is rigged. Pull your money from the pot and come along."

At once the stillness settled in.

The three riggers stared up at Buck. The two of them who were the flankers looked at the lead man sitting opposite J.C. The lead man shook off the signal for a shoot-out and said to Buck quietly, "What did you say, boy?"

The easiness of the voice warned Buck. He knew immediately that he had walked into a trap. That he was standing on a hair-trigger baitpan. That if he so much as breathed the wrong word he would spring the steel jaws shut on himself.

"I meant to say," he began, "that my friend here is in no shape to play with—well, that is—he ought not to have—"

"You are right," interrupted the quiet man. "He ought not to have. Anything else you want to say, boy?"

Before Buck could flounder in any deeper, J.C. blew up. He called Buck down in gutter language which would, and did, embarrass him in front of a street girl. Buck blushed deeply but did not know what to do about J.C., the cussing out, or any of it. In the end, he stepped back, palming his hands to show the riggers he had no intention of pulling his gun and was dragging his bet. Since it *was* a crooked game the sharpers did not press for apologies but played out the hand without another glance for the Samaritan who had felt the call, so chillingly and in such good time, to go preach elsewhere.

Nonetheless, Buck had done his damage. In the time it took J.C. to lose the final hand, he began to sober up and think back over the way the game had gone. In consequence, when the lead rigger laid down a straight flush in diamonds to beat J.C.'s beautiful queens-over-aces full, J.C. called him a four-flushing son of a bitch and made his move to steal the pot with his pistol.

His fast gun never cleared leather.

The two flankers shot him from under the table, the right-hand man twice, the left-hand one, three times. He half turned in his chair, threw Buck a pale, frightened look and groaned softly, "Buck, you was right. I'm sorry. Oh, God, it does hurt." Then he clamped his hands to his stomach, slid under the table and was dead in the time it took Buck to pull his own gun and hear his voice saying calmly, "All right you three bastards—hands on the wood and don't breathe."

The riggers looked up for their second appraisal of the homely red-headed boy with the arid West Texas drawl and did not like it nearly so well as the first. Their hands came up empty, obediently and quick.

"You," said Buck to the girl, "count out fifty dollars in greenbacks and put it where it came from—my vest pocket."

The girl sized him up a moment, then did as she was bid. While she was about it, Buck told the riggers the story of J.C. and the money and invited them to follow him out and take it back should they feel they had it coming. The three professionals shook their heads to show him they did not harbor any such unfriendly notions. Odds were a business with them. Right now this tall, rough-cut kid held the house edge. Let him enjoy it. They had the proper connections in town. They could wait.

"Forget it, kid," said the lead man, not unkindly. "Cash out and go home while you're ahead."

Buck nodded just as the girl announced, "Here's your fifty, mister," and slipped the folded bills into the pocket of his sheepskin vest. She started away but Buck called out sharply, "Hold on, I ain't done with you yet. Count out thirty of those cartwheel dollars from the pot." The girl shrugged, went back to the table, began sliding out and stacking the big coins. When she had pulled and piled the thirty silver pieces, she turned to Buck questioningly.

"Pick 'em up," he told her. "They're for you."

"For me?" She frowned. "What for?"

"Remember Judas in the Bible, miss?" he asked her. "The same wages for the same work."

He saw her painted face go pale and he nodded and touched the wide, bent-curled brim of his hat and went out of the saloon into the street. He did not look back and did not think he needed to.

He was right. No one chose to follow him.

13   Preferring of Charges

BUCK FOUND the town marshal's office just down the street. He went in, found the marshal unoccupied, nodded politely and said, "Excuse me, sir, my name is Buck Burnet. What does a first-class funeral cost in this town?"

The marshal, an older, white-haired man, did not miss a drag on his Spanish cigarette.

"Ten dollars for a pine box, twenty-five for the undertaker, ten for the hole-digger and the headboard, five for the preacher."

Buck frowned, losing his politeness.

"God always gets the short end, don't he?" he said.

"Never heard him complain," shrugged the marshal. "Why should you?"

"I ain't. You said fifty dollars all told?"

"I didn't say it but that's what it comes to."

Buck took out the wad of bills, threw them on the desk.

"There's a dead boy up at the Golden Calf," he said. "Got cut down in a crooked poker game. Should have held onto his mouth instead of his openers. I would be beholden, Marshal, if you would see he gets a good service."

"Friend of yours, son?"

"I didn't say it but that's what it comes to."

The old marshal took the slim cheroot from his mouth.

"You get fresh with me, kid, you're in trouble. Don't try it." He flicked an ash without taking his gaze from the Concho boy's freckled face. "This town ain't too partial to Texicans to start off with. Was I you, I wouldn't be adding deliberate to the score."

"I didn't come in here for advice," said Buck. "You going to take the money and see to those services or not?"

"You ain't showed me yet where I should take it," said the old man, still watching him closely.

Buck reached for the money but the old man reached quicker than he did.

"All right," he said, "you just showed me." He picked up the money, stuffed it in his pocket. "I will need some information on the deceased," he announced, wetting a stub of lead pencil. "Fire away, but not too swift. I ain't no court reporter."

Buck told him his own full name, where he was from, and who J.C. was and where he was from. As well, he told him how to address the latter's parents in Menard County so that he could write them and tell them about the death of their son, which duty the old lawman quietly accepted. Buck then concluded tersely. "I got his horse and rigging outside. The horse is a goosey paint and not worth shooting but will fetch forty dollars from some dude who wants to put on a show for the locals. Saddle is hand-tooled Mexican on a Pecos tree and will bring sixty-five from the first rider you want to stop in the street. My friend carried an old thirty-six caliber Colt's Navy which I would like to keep, and you can bury him in his clothes."

The old marshal looked up at him. "What for you telling me all this, kid?" he asked almost plaintively.

"I thought likely you could sell the stuff and send the money on to his folks with the letter. They ain't rich, Marshal. You say the word, I will just leave his horse and rigging at the rail."

The old man got up from the desk, the little moment of near-warmth dissipated. "You will leave them there anyway," he said frostily. "They are city property now and will go at auction."

"By God!" Buck started to object, but the leathery-faced lawman waved his anger aside with a warning jab of the cigarette.

"Kid," he said, "you shut your damned mouth and you get out of here. I got to figure myself in on these things, I ain't no choice. Otherwise the job don't pay enough to feed a man three squares."

"Now listen here, Marshal," Buck began again, but again he was waved down.

"No," said the other, "you listen. I'm going to give you the best advice you ever had in your life." He paused, worrying the small cigar back to life, and swept quickly ahead as the blue smoke curled.

"Here's the way it is, kid, believe it. You're from out of state and you ain't no friends in Shreveport. You ain't the money to go bail nor put up a bribe and there's nothing but your word for who you are and how come your friend to get killed. You're mixed up with a bunch of sharks from the rottenest-run saloon north of New Orleans. Now that's about your side of it, here's mine.

"I don't like you Texas saddle tramps moving through my town on your way to the war. You ain't none of you ever got a damned dime to spend and you always wind up signing your saloon checks with a sixgun to cover the shortage. We got a circuit court runs twenty-four hours a day just to handle the wartime traffic from your state alone. And we got a hanging judge riding its bench who don't cotton a Yankee damn to cowboys from west of Red River.

"Now you come up in front of this cantankery old son of a bitch for so much as spitting on the sidewalk and I will guarantee that you will draw thirty days. Drunk and disorderly will get you three months minimum, with a hundred and twenty days if you open your mouth more than enough to say thank you for the three months. Accessory to the fact, in a fatal shooting like this one, will earn you a year and a day in the state penitentiary. . . . Boy!" he wound up, jabbing once more at Buck with the cigarillo, "are you reading my smoke?"

He accepted Buck's respectful head bob, went on quickly.

"You get out of this town, son, and you keep going fast and far. I know that outfit up to the Golden Calf. They will be in here swearing out a warrant for your arrest before you can say Sam Houston. They can't afford anybody running around loose claiming the house odds get company help at the Calf. Bad as hell for business. On the other hand, what some bum in jail claims don't hurt trade none at all. You get the drift, boy?"

Buck got the drift. He was grateful for the warning but still indignant about it, too.

"Sure, Marshal," he said. "But damn it all, I didn't do nothing myself!"

"You got any witnesses will swear you didn't?"

"Sure, there was that girl. She . . ."

"She," the old man took up for him, "is a house shill and a streetwalker. Any witnessing she does for you will only bang the bars shut on you that much longer. She will be retired and running her own call house before you get your sentence half served. Smarten up, kid, and start moving."

Buck began backing out of the office. He kept on backing until he was in the street and grabbing for his gelding's reins. Then he remembered his manners.

"Thanks, Marshal," he called back. "I surely do owe you one."

"Get!" snapped the white-haired lawman, coming to stand in the lamplight of the door. "And don't do no looking back. Something might be gaining on you."

Buck put his spurs to the steeldust and went off up the street at a rocking gallop. The old man stood watching after him a long time. At last he turned away.

"That," he announced to the four walls of the office, "is what I get for being brung up in Texas. I ought to have took the young rooster for every cent he had. Yes, and throwed him in jail till he could write home for more. But, oh no, not me. I got to go and turn sentimental and get to thinking of them God-blessed times in the Trinity bottoms when I wasn't no older than him."

He sat down heavily, shaking his head and still growling, but growling soft and sad and happy, the way an old man will when something has returned him for a golden moment to boyhood.

"Jesus, but a gingery kid like that does take a man back," he said. "Dear God Almighty, it's been near forty years. . . ."

At the barn Buck did not fare so well. The boys were badly shaken up by the news of J.C.'s death. Somehow, they blamed Buck for it. He had been the one to take over the lead and call himself captain. That put him in line to be the one to humble J.C., and didn't that make him responsible for what followed? It was Little Bit Luckett, the dead boy's cousin, who put the answer to the unasked question into words for the rest of the troop.

"Maybe," said Little Bit, "if you hadn't of poked your nose into the game, he wouldn't have lost nothing but the money. What you honestly think, Buck?"

Buck bowed his head. He did not want to look at any of them and he could not look at Little Bit. But there was no crawling out from under it. The load was his and he might as well pick it up and tote it for what it weighed. The situation was entirely different from the one with Cart Amon. Cart's injury was an act of the Lord. It had forced Buck into risking Cart's life, but rightly so. With J.C. the Lord hadn't had a hand in it. All that remained for Buck Burnet was to be a man and admit as much.

He raised his lowered glance, catching Little Bit's puzzled gaze and holding it steadily.

"You know what I honestly think, Tobin Earl?" he said. "I think you're right."

14   Final Orders

LATE THAT NIGHT the marshal showed up at the barn and took Buck on a charge of armed robbery. It was a running iron accusation, he admitted. There were times, he said, when his job got pretty gamey. But it was his job and a man ate what he had to eat when he was crowding sixty and his teeth were gone.

Buck was not given time to say good-bye. He did manage to call to Miller to take command, go ahead and sell the horses, buy the tickets for Vicksburg and get on to Richmond without worrying about him, Buck. Then the marshal was poking him with his shotgun and saying, "All right, boy, let's go. You can make the rest of your farewell address from the alley window of the city jail."

In town he was given a midnight trial and a year and a day in the state penitentiary by the villainous circuit judge about whom the marshal had warned him. Remanded to the marshal's custody, he was led away half believing he deserved his sentence and was possibly lucky not to have drawn thirty years on the rockpile. The midnight hours at the jail wore away lonesomely and chill. It was nearing 2:00 A.M., with Buck pining mournfully out the window of his cell, when Miller Nalls hallooed him from out of the cross-alley shadows and inquired earnestly, "Hey, Buck, what the hell you doing in there?"

It was just the innocent, dumb kind of a question you could expect from Miller but in this case it cheered Buck not at all.

"I'm writing my memoirs," he called back, "but I can't seem to think up enough dirty words to get started. What the hell you doing out there?"

"Well," said Miller proudly, "we been busy."

"Come over here where I can see you," ordered Buck. "There ain't nobody going to bite you. The deputy's off duty and the marshal's snoring fit to shake the bars loose." At this, Miller and the rest of the boys crept cautiously across the alley and Buck said sharply to Miller, "All right, what things you really been getting done?"

"Well," said the latter, "first off I done assumed the command like you told me. Then I sold the horses. Then I went and asked about them stage and train tickets to Vicksburg. But it seemed we was one fare short of having enough to pay for the six of us to ride the whole way, so the boys said the hell with it, we would get old Buck a Philadelphia lawyer to crook his way out of jail and then worry about getting on to Richmond after that. You reckon I done good so far, Buck?"

"You got the lawyer yet?" demanded Buck sternly.

"Well, no, we ain't."

"Then you done good. Now you all listen to me."

Quickly he told them of his sentence in the state penitentiary. They might as well realize, he said, that they would have to go on without him. There was a good side to that, too, he added, for without him they would have just the right amount of money to buy the five tickets they would need. Immediately they tried to cut in on him but he would not listen to their objections. He had one last order to give them; after that Miller would be the captain and they would take their orders from him. Meanwhile, Buck asked them to remember they were the Concho County Comanches and to let the pride of that go with them into every battle they faced in freeing the South from the vile yoke of Yankee unionism.

It was quite a speech for a seventeen-year-old boy who had yet to see his first Confederate soldier. It very nearly brought his young followers to tears and for an embarrassing moment their throats were too tight to risk any back talk. Then the reaction set in.

"Now damn it to hell, Buck," Eubie began, "we don't aim to do it and we ain't agoing to do it!"

"You don't aim and you ain't going to do what?" asked Buck quietly.

"Well, whatever the hell it is you're saving that there last order of yours for!" answered the other boy defiantly. But before the revolt could spread, Miller broke in and said, "Say, Buck, we got one other little problem we ain't told you about. We figured you'd have the answer for it, so we brung it along."

"Well," said Buck, cooling off both from his oration and Eubie's uprising, "you come to the right place. This just happens to be my night for small problems. So whatever you got of them, boys, big or little, drag 'em on out and let old Buck settle them."

He had not expected his acid comment to be taken literally, but it was. Big Todo, who had been standing behind the others, stepped forward.

"Here it is," said Todo laconically. "Caught up to us at the barn and wouldn't take 'get the hell back to the swamp' for an answer. Said you told him he could go along if he asked his folks' permission."

"My God," gasped Buck, "I was only funning with him!"

"Yup," said Eubie Buell. "But he wasn't funning with you."

Buck looked down through the bars.

"Pablo," he demanded accusingly, "you sure you asked your folks' permission?"

"Yes sir, *Capitán!*"

"Pablo," he said seriously, "do you mean to stand there on your word as a Massanet, a man whose father lost an arm at Cerro Cordo, and tell me your folks give you permission to come shagging off after us?"

The boy drew himself erect.

"No sir," he answered. "My father and my mother they both thought I must be *loco* to imagine they would agree to such a thing."

"Well, then," exclaimed Buck victoriously, "you've no right to be here and you will simply have to turn around and march back home!"

"No, *Capitán,* that is not to our understanding," denied the other. "You said only that it was necessary to *ask* permission; you did not say that it was necessary to receive it."

Buck swore under his breath, appealed openly for an honorable solution, was furnished one by Eubie Buell.

"No need to go back on your word, Buck," he said, "nor incriminate the reputation of the Concho County Comanches. We got money for only five tickets on that stage to Vicksburg. I reckon that leaves the Weasel in Shreveport fair and square."

Buck did not argue the opportunity, but seized upon it. "By Jings, that's so," he said, then added hopefully to the boy, "you can see that, can't you, Pablo?"

If young Massanet could see it, he was not ready to admit as much. He fervently proclaimed instead that he would be Buck's constant shadow, the troop's mess servant and stablehand to the horses, that he would go three days without food, march a week without shoes, sleep without blankets in the rain, stand watch all of every night, anything absolutely anything, if he might only be permitted to go with the company. In the end Buck had to get harsh with him, putting his instruction to return home in the form of a military command. The swamp boy reacted as though Buck had struck him in the back with a dagger. He could not hide the shine of his tears, nor the tremble in his voice.

"Very well, *Capitán*," he said. "If it is an order, what can a man do?"

Wheeling to face the mute Comanches, he said, *"Vayan con Dios, amigos,"* and marched off down the alley. When he was gone and when the guilty silence had lasted long enough, Miller cleared his throat.

"Well, Buck," he said remindfully, "what was that there last order you was talking about?"

"Just this," said Buck, talking quickly and crisply to make it sound official, "when that 2:30 stage pulls out I want you all aboard her and no arguments. *That's an order.* Now I mean it, boys, and you must not think of me but only of your duty to your country and your vows as Comanches. I want your words on it. They will hold me proud while we're apart."

There was no vestige of rebellion remaining in the stillness which followed. The silence of his friends was simply their tribute to Buck's courage. They looked at him, all of them standing tall in the moonlight, and he looked back at them in the same way. No one said a word and it was a wonderful moment. There wasn't a dry eye in the alley. Then Miller Nalls asked shakily, "Was there anything else, Buck?" and Buck answered, "No, only good luck and God bless you one and all." Miller waited another awkward moment, then gave their leader the first effort at a formal salute any of them had attempted.

"Yes, sir," he said, and wheeled about and marched away down the alley. The others went after him, saluting and marching stiff as tin past Buck's window. At the corner of the jail building Miller hung back to count his new command by. When they had all gone safely out of hearing he looked back and called low-voiced to Buck. "Good-bye, Buck, we will do you fearful proud when we get to Richmond . . .!"

15   Retreat by the River

THE MOON RODE LOW over the misting bottomlands. Outside the jail it was so quiet Buck could hear the swirl of the brown water cutting against the levee at the foot of the alley. He could see the broad bend of the Red River from his cell window, and could hear the low singing of the Negro dockhands loading some trim packet for her daybreak run down to the Mississippi. The singing was the sweetest, most lonely sound he had ever heard. It made him sad and restless to listen to it. He looked away from the river, up the alley, toward the corner around which Miller and the boys had disappeared.

It seemed a year since they had gone. He knew it was more like an hour, though, and that they had still not left town. Buck moved away from the window. At the cell door he could see just enough of the outer office to make out the marshal's boots propped on the desk and the looping of J.C.'s gunbelt hung on a wall peg beyond the desk. The marshal, hearing him stir about, called in testily.

"That you, boy? Why don't you bed down in there? What you trying to do, work on my conscience?"

Buck did not answer him at first but after a bit he said, "Marshal, you ever been in jail?"

"Never been much of any place else. Been around jails the last thirty years."

"I don't mean around. I mean inside."

"I done six months once. You want a cup of coffee, boy? It's hot."

"What for, Marshal? The six months, I mean."

"Stealing a bag of flint corn."

"Why did you do it?"

"We was hog poor. It fed us. Kept us going."

"What was it like, the six months?"

"Hell's fire, how would I remember? That was thirty-five years ago. You want that coffee, boy?"

"Yes, sir, I'd like some now, thank you. You mind talking, Marshal? I don't want to bother you."

The old man's boots disappeared off the desk top and the legs of his wireback chair scraped on the stone floor. He came into the cell block carrying the chair like a tray, the coffeepot and two tin cups balanced on its caned seat.

"You're not bothering anybody, boy," he said. "But if you want to talk you had better get to doing it. My deputy is coming on duty in a few minutes. Jules is a close-mouthed man, and young. He wears his badge but wants mine. I doubt he will listen to you."

Buck nodded his thanks. He took the coffee as it was handed in through the bars, and said, "Marshal, I've been thinking."

"So have I," said the old man, watching him.

Buck wondered about the look, then went on.

"Tell me just one thing, Marshal. Tonight, up yonder in that saloon, three grown men shot and killed a green boy. They crossfired him under the table. He never had a chance. Now wasn't that murder?"

The old man shook his head. "He was wearing a gun and he went for it," he said.

"But it was a rigged game, they was cheating!"

"Life ain't run under no other rules."

"You know they murdered my friend, then?"

"There's little doubt of it."

"Yet here I am on my way to the penitentiary for taking fifty dollars that was mine to begin with. And there they are free as the air for killing an innocent person in cold blood."

"Boy, I told you the game don't pay off on who's right and who's wrong. It's who gets caught that counts."

"In this case me," said Buck bitterly.

"In this case you," agreed the marshal.

He was quiet for a minute, pulling at his faded mustaches and staring out the alley window. Then, grimacing, he went on. "But once in a great spell there's a damned old mutton-headed fool gets himself into the middle of the game where he ain't no business being. Then maybe the odds change a mite and the cheaters get cheated on. No matter, though, it's still somebody cheating that steals the pot."

"I allow you lost me, Marshal," frowned Buck. "I thought we was talking about me."

"And me," said the old man softly.

Buck waited, then, and finally the marshal, after another interminable look out the window, made his point.

"It's your lucky night, kid. We're alone in the jail and you make me homesick for Texas. Likewise, you set me to thinking about thirty-five, forty years I don't know what become of. You know something, boy? When I was your age I had red hair, too. Yes, and my ways and feelings was just as free and stirred up as yours, or as any wild kid's what's growed up in the pear thickets of the *brasada*, or out on the buffler grass of the *llano*."

He got up abruptly, went out into the office. He left the coffeepot on the floor but took the chair with him. He was back in a moment, the cell block key ring in one hand, J.C.'s gunbelt in the other. Opening Buck's cell he handed him the gunbelt.

"Hurry up," he said. "Jules will be here directly."

Buck followed him, wise enough not to ask questions. In the office, the old man crossed to the street door, which he opened. Peering out, he nodded. "Coast is clear, let's go." Then he led the way through a side door into a vacant building adjoining the jail. Through the musty darkness of this structure they felt their way to a third door, which opened, again, on the jail alley. The marshal pointed down the alley toward the levee.

"You leg it down yonder to the river, kid," he said. "Skirt along it through the cottonwoods till you're free of town. Then rent or steal yourself a boat from one of them levee darkies and get on over the stream. Once acrost, swing back up north to cut the Vicksburg road a mile or so east. Stage should be along by the time you get there." He pulled out his watch. "It's 2:10 now. Stage schedule calls for a 2:30 departure. Jules is due on duty at 2:45. It's cutting it awful fine but there ain't a damned thing else I can do for you, saving maybe this." He pulled out a roll of paper bills—a mighty familiar roll of them—and pressed it into Buck's hand. "Here's your money back, boy. Long as you're breaking jail you might as well take the state's evidence with you. Now leg it, and don't look back!"

"Marshal," Buck began, "how on earth you ever going to make this look right from your end?"

But the old man waved him down angrily. "Don't you worry about my end!" he snapped. "Get on your way!"

"Yes sir, Marshal. I'll pay you back one day."

"Get!" rasped the old man. "Goddam it, I told you I done six months when I was a kid."

"Yes, sir," said Buck, "and you had red hair."

"Red as sin," muttered the marshal.

Buck gestured with his hand, afraid to speak his farewell aloud, and started to walk away. In a moment he was trotting. Then, suddenly, he was running for dear life. He never did turn to look back and the old marshal didn't wait to see if he did. As he had said, Jules was an edgy devil. If he showed up for work more than five minutes early, the red-headed kid was as dead as his friend in the Golden Calf.

Back in the jail office the old man opened the street door just wide enough so that he could sit at his desk and see down the main stem. At 2:35 he heard the Vicksburg stage pull out and smiled and drew deep on his cigarette and drank the rest of the coffee in his cup. At 2:40 he saw Jules coming down the boardwalk and got up quickly and went into the cell block. With a second smile, more of a grin than the first, he dropkicked the coffeepot against the stone wall with a clanging splash. In the same moment, he flung wide the door to Buck's cell, gave an Indian yell and ran out into the front office. There he grabbed his shotgun, fired one barrel into the coal-oil lamp overhead, the other through the dirty glass of a side window. The gun still smoking, he ran into the street yelling for help and cursing the natural kindness which had led him to take coffee to the Texas kid's cell and be careless enough not to keep a close watch of the young scoundrel while doing it.

Thirty minutes later the old marshal and his tough young deputy rode north up the Red River toward the Arkansas line, at the head of a sandy-eyed posse. Two miles east of Shreveport, a polite red-headed Texas boy, somewhat mud spattered and out of breath but clutching fifty good dollars in Union paper money in his left hand and a wide-brimmed Concho sombrero in his right, had just stepped out of the early morning drizzle to flag down the Vicksburg stage. Subsequently the red-headed boy met with such a welcome of glad bear hugs and coyote yips from the other Texas youths on the stage, as to incline the veteran driver to believe he had picked up a very important passenger.

16 Munroe Station

THE COACH was a new nine-passenger Abbott & Downing, the horses full of run, the roadbed good all the way. Rocketing past Sparta and Burtonville, they pulled the forty-eight miles to Middleton in five hours. The Comanches disembarked, their appetites as high and hearty as their spirits. Breakfast was no more than enjoyed, however, when their driver appeared in the stationhouse doorway.

"Which one of you Texas heroes," he challenged, "belongs to that duffel sack in the boot?"

The Comanches stared at one another.

"Which duffel sack was that?" inquired Todo.

"The one that was stowed just as we was leaving Shreveport." The driver peered more closely at Todo. "Matter of fact," he said, "*you* was the one that stowed it."

"Me?" said Todo.

"You," said the driver.

"Oh, *that* duffel sack," said Todo. "I'm downright glad you mentioned it, driver. I was just going to tell the boys about it."

"Well, don't bother. Jim, bring that sack in here."

The station hostler appeared dragging a large canvas kit bag across the floor. He halted in front of the driver, who pointed angrily at the sack.

"You know what's in there?" he demanded of the Comanches.

"Duffel, I suppose," offered Eubie. "Seeing's how it's a duffel sack."

"Real wise, ain't you?" said the driver. "You ever get bit by a duffel sack?" He held up a puffed thumb. "I just did. Leave me tell you it's a shock."

"Whatever happened?" asked Buck mildly.

"You tell me," fumed the driver. "Jim and me was just now putting the new passenger's valise in the boot out yonder when I seen this here damned sack start to move. I reached down for it and, by God, it bit me. Jim, empty it out. Careful you don't get grabbed."

Jim nodded, taking hold of the sack cautiously. With a sudden heave he upended it and jumped back, spilling its contents upon the floor.

"Good Lord amercy!" cried Buck.

"*Si, Capitán,*" admitted Pablo Massanet. "It is I. I am here."

They could not argue the fact. Eubie performed his customary service of supplying the company opinion.

"Welcome to the Comanches, Weasel," he said. "Stand up and be swore in."

"Now wait just a minute," said the driver. "What you aim to do about his fare? He can't ride free. He'll go half-fare or he won't go at all. That goes either way, whether you send him back or take him on with you."

"Mister," appealed Buck, "we're stony broke. Couldn't you close your eyes far as the traincars at Munroe Station? We ain't the money either to send him home or take him along. What you say?"

"I say leave him right here!" scowled the driver.

"Well, Todo," said Buck, "it was your idea to sack him up and ship him. What do you say?"

Todo bobbed his head, stepped over to the driver.

"I say the kid goes along with us to Munroe Station. Now you think about that real hard, mister."

"Yes, sir," said Willy Bill, leading the general troop movement to encircle the cornered driver. "You do that and let us know how she figures to you on second shot."

The driver ran his eyes over the tall, rawboned youngsters. He licked his lips, pouting the stubble on his chin.

"You boys trying to buffalo me?" he demanded.

"Yes, sir," replied Willy Bill politely. "We surely are."

"Mr. Decker," said Jim, the station hostler, "there ain't nobody here today saving me and you and the cook. Agent Bowden and his missus done gone inter Munroe fer supplies."

"Three against six," announced Todo, as the driver lost color around the gills. "It don't hardly seem fair."

"Not six, but seven, *señor*," corrected Pablo proudly, and stepped over to stand beside his huge benefactor.

Eubie studied the comparison in altitudes, fingering his chin. Finally, he shook his head. "Six and a half is all I can give you, Weasel," he said. "You don't come no more than hipbone high to a mired duck."

Whatever the odds, they were enough. After threatening legal redress in Munroe, the driver said no more. Pablo got aboard with the Comanches. A last-minute tactical decision involving the empty duffel sack was quickly made by Buck. "Bring it along," he told Todo. "I got an idea the railroad ain't going to be any more open-handed than this here stageline." Todo grinned in agreement. "I reckon you're right, Buck," he said. "Besides, look at the size of him." He picked up Pablo with one hand. "He don't weigh no more than Little Bit's watch, or a pancake saddle, and a body never knows when he might have need of a first-class weasel."

"That's true," said Buck. "Put him in your pocket and let's go."

The passenger coming on the stage at Middleton proved a fine host for the Texas boys. He was a native of the area, a small planter and a hot secessionist. When he discovered where they were from, and where bound, he produced a pint bottle of sourmash bourbon and insisted on standing the crowd. He did not have to insist overlong and his pint was gone almost before he got it out of his waistcoat.

Shortly, everything looked better to the Comanches, even garrulous "Colonel" Mirabeau Cooney. The glow lasted to within three miles of Munroe Station, Louisiana, at which point a roadblock of local whites armed with long-barreled shotguns was encountered.

"Runaway nigger," said Colonel Cooney without hesitation. "They try busting loose from us to get over the Red into Texas. Not many make it, though, and this one sure never will."

"How so?" asked Buck, more to be courteous than because of any real interest. A runaway slave seemed reasonable enough and certainly not a serious matter.

"That there's Case Pettibone yonder at the barricade. Overseer for old General Gainesford's fieldhands. They don't none of them get away from Case."

"I believe it," said Buck, looking out the window as the stage halted and Case Pettibone, shotgun held in the crook of his bony arm, lounged forward. "He just plain looks ornery."

"It's his job," said the Colonel. "You don't run close to a hundred nigras at hard field work with a kind smile. Not ever."

Outside, Buck heard the stage driver call down to the overseer, "How many you running this time, Case?" and then the overseer answering, "Just one. Big blue buck. About thirty or so. Mean one. We're close to him, though. Dogs are cutting trail just ahead. Likely you'll hear 'em open up 'fore you hit Munroe."

"Sure. We'll keep an eye out, Case," said the driver. "How's your old lady?"

"Some better. Still puny for real work. She'll gain. You see this nigra up ahead, Decker, you pull two shots. We got dogs both sides of the road. One pack or the other will pick up your signal and come in. Hear?"

"Sure thing, Case. Stand clear, I'm running late. *Hee-yahh,* Becky, Pete, Blackie, Queen—*shoo-ahh . . . !*"

The teams hit their tugs hard. The whip of the big coach on its leather thoroughbraces spilled Little Bit and Pablo on the floor with Todo on top of them and in the resulting laugh the blockade halt was forgotten. But just forgotten. A mile along the road, in a stretch of piney woods and huckleberry bramble, the boys heard, and shortly saw, a pack of Redbone hounds running full bell on a hot track. As they leaned to look out the coach windows on Buck's side, the dogs' quarry burst from the timber. It was the runaway fieldhand.

He saw the stage and its interested passengers and at once came crying toward it, pleading for the good people to stop and save him from the dogs.

"God A'mighty," said Miller Nalls to Buck, "the pore thing is afeared for his life. He's scairt wall-eyed!" Buck's blunt jaw set up angrily. "He sure is," he said. "Why ain't the driver stopping?"

"To pick up that nigra?" said Colonel Cooney in surprise. "Not quite today, boys. He's dog bait for sure. Those are Ben Swasey's Redbones running yonder. Ben won't be far behind. They'll have that black scoundrel heeled and hamstrung before he makes timber again. Watch close now."

"No, sir, by God," said Buck Burnet softly, "*you* watch close." With the words he twisted his long body out the window of the swaying coach. Seizing the baggage rail, he hauled himself up to the roofdeck above. There he rolled to the seatbox, palming out J.C.'s Navy Colt on the roll and slamming its muzzle into the driver's ribs. His voice was as soft as it had been below, but it was the sort of softness which stopped stagecoaches.

"Now then, you slack-jawed son of a bitch," he said, "you haul back on them horses."

The driver took one look at him and sat the wheel team on its haunches. The stage nosedived, leveled out, stopped dead. The colored man leaped for the wheel hub, reaching to take Buck's hand. Buck heaved upward, almost throwing the terrified Negro onto the roofdeck.

"Get going," he told the driver. "And don't lay an ounce of drag on them lines till I tell you to."

By this time the hounds had broken free of the woods and were nearly to the road. Behind them, at timber's edge, five lanky white men stood poised, their eyes sweeping to the moving stage.

"Hold on there!" one of them brawled. "You cain't make off with that nigra, he's a runaway!"

Buck, never quick with words, had no answer for the man. But Eubie had. "Yes, sir, we know he is," he shouted back, "but he's our runaway now." Then, leaning to his belt buckle out of the lurching coach and yelling it at lungs' top, "Whyn't you try running *us* down with them goddam dawgs, you Loozy-anna sons of bitches?"

Past the first bend out of sight of the hound-dog men, Buck ordered the driver to pull up. Detailing Todo to take over the reins and not to stop for anything less than a rifle shot, he herded the driver and the colored man into the stage below.

For a misguided moment Colonel Cooney believed he was going to make trouble. He began to declaim sonorously that he would not ride in the same conveyance with any Negro alive. Buck quietly told him that he saw it differently. He was not, he said, of a mind or nature to take kindly to seeing human beings, black, brown, blue, or any other color that Colonel Mirabeau Cooney might want to mention, being run by dogs. In this case, Colonel Cooney was not only going to ride with a colored man but was going to keep his damned mouth shut while doing so. If he didn't like the pucker of those persimmons he had just better sit there and wince to himself. For, like it or let it lay, they were taking this poor fellow into Munroe Station and giving him safely over to the proper authorities. In that way he would be returned to his owner in a decent, lawful manner, not hounded down in the woods like some helpless animal.

At this statement the Negro, who until that moment had been watching Buck with a half-fearful, half-worshipful look, gave a low moan and buried his face in his hands. Glancing at him, puzzled, Eubie frowned and said, "What's the matter with him? I should think he would be glad to be give his full protection of the legal law."

The colonel, recovering from Buck's warning, gestured forgivingly. "Oh, it's not that, young friend," he said. "It's simply that he doesn't understand what you're trying to do for him. These nigras are like small children. Expecting punishment for wrongdoing, they exaggerate their fears out of all proportion. They are pathetically lacking in the basic intellect, you see. More like dumb brutes then intelligent beings in the levels of their abilities to comprehend. Naturally, we appreciate this deficiency and give them the utmost tolerance and good treatment in view of it, you may believe me. As for this rascal, his indulgent owner—I know the old General well—will no doubt let him off with a light lecture and perhaps a lash or two."

Now the Negro's eyes rolled to Buck again. His lips struggled but no speech came forth. Buck put a hand on his knee and said to him gently, "Now go easy, you hear? Talk up when you're a mind to. And you can say what you want. You ain't nothing to fear from us."

"Lawd Gawd, boy," burst out the man, "it hain't you I got to fear, it's de law you gwine ter turn me over to. If de High Sherff in Munroe git his hands on me, I hain't never gwine git back to Ol' Gen'r'l. Fur as you go, de Lawd will bless you, young master. He will! He will!"

"We're not your masters," said Buck. "We're just seeing you get to town safe. The High Sheriff ain't going to harm you none, either. I'll talk to him myself, if you want."

The Negro man shook his head. He didn't answer Buck, but began muttering softly to himself. Listening to him, Buck grew very uneasy. He turned to Eubie and whispered, "Say, I believe he's praying, ain't he?" and Eubie looked at the man and said, "Sure enough he is. The poor feller ain't in his right mind, Buck."

"Indeed," broke in Colonel Cooney, "that is precisely the case. And if you boys will give him into the custody of Sheriff Slocum in Munroe you will be doing him the greatest kindness. As a matter of fact, I am getting off at Munroe myself and will undertake to deliver him to Slocum if you wish me to." He paused, eyeing the Concho boys deliberately. "It might not be too bad an idea, at that, my young Texas friends," he said, "in view of your interference back yonder. I can say a few words to the sheriff and the incident will be closed. I might advise you to consider it rather carefully."

"Young master," said the colored man in his soft voice, "if you let de High Sherff have me, dey will kill me sho. Dey will lie and say I done touch a white lady, or some other killin' thing, and dey will see I doan git home. I run off twice before, and dis is de las' time. You gonter give me over to the High Sherff, boy, dey will kill me 'fore dat yar train pull clear de Munroe depot."

"Oh, that ain't so," objected Buck. "It couldn't be."

"Of course not," smiled Colonel Cooney. "You leave the matter to me, boys. You have my word as a gentleman and a Southerner that no harm will come to the rascal."

"Lawd Gawd, doan do it, boy, doan do it," muttered the runaway. "Stop de coach and leave me run agin. Mebbe I kin make it dis time. Ise rested some an' de dawgs hain't so close. Stop de coach, white boy. Praise be to Gawd, stop de hosses an' leave me run agin!"

"We can't do that," said Buck. "We can't put you down to be run by them dawgs again."

The colored man nodded. He turned away from Buck and stared out the coach window. His lips began to move, soundlessly at first, then with a strangely beautiful underbreath melody issuing from them. The haunting cadences kept time with the slow swaying of his body and sightless nodding of his kinky, sweat-streaked head. Miller Nalls grimaced and glanced apprehensively at Buck.

"You know what he's doing, Buck? He's singing a hymn. 'Rock of Ages,' ain't it? Listen . . ."

Both boys inclined their heads, the others watching them, a peculiar silence growing in the coach. Even Colonel Mirabeau Cooney held his peace. Presently Buck nodded and said half aloud, "Yes, that's it, sure enough."

Miller shivered, hunching unconsciously away from the far-eyed prisoner. The latter did not notice. He no longer remembered he was in the coach with the white boys. His mind and heart were traveling with his gaze, out and beyond any ken of theirs.

> "Rock of Ages, cleft for me,
> Let me hide myself in Thee . . ."

17 Colonel Cooney's Word

THEY CAME INTO MUNROE STATION AT 2:00 P.M. The settlement, railhead of the Vicksburg & Shreveport Railroad, was swarming with local traffic. This stir, mainly of farm vehicles engaged in transhipment of forage supplies to the front-line military depots, was the Comanches' first visual proof that the war was still very much alive. In response to this excitement their eagerness to be aboard the railroad cars mounted intolerably. Buck held them down.

Before arrival, he had decided to take advantage of Colonel Cooney's offer, letting the planter deliver the Negro to Sheriff Slocum and also use his personal influence with the officer to see that nothing serious was made of the Comanches' interference with the manhunt outside Munroe. Now he decided he would go along with the Colonel to make certain the colored man *was* given over to the proper authorities and that the latter *would* treat him as Cooney had intimated. It was, he thought, the least he could do for the poor fellow.

He found High Sheriff Slocum a middle-aged man of quite reasonable, even kindly disposition. The officer told him that, indeed, some example had to be made of runaway fieldhands. It was necessary, he said, to serve as fair and decent warning to their fellows who might be tempted to try the same thing. However, and despite the fact this par-

ticular fellow had twice before attempted escape, he would
get no more punishment than he properly deserved. With
sincere, fatherly warmth he further advised Buck to forget
the entire occurrence, being easy in his mind about it and
going on to Richmond with good heart and clear conscience,
satisfied he had done his lawful and moral duty in returning
the man.

This good news, brought back to the Comanches by a
vastly relieved Buck Burnet, struck just the right tone.

"You done fine, Buck," said Eubie, for once serious. "To
tell you the truth I was downright worried about that colored
man. Now I reckon we can all climb aboard them cars
yonder, without no indubitable concerns."

The others nodded their certain convictions that this was
so, yet to see them, presently, shying away from and circling
around the little wooden passenger coach which would bear
them on to Vicksburg, made it difficult to imagine they meant
it. Watching them, Buck had to smile. But it was a com-
miserating smile, not a superior one, for he was shying right
with them, no more anxious to be the first to assault the high
steps to the car's vestibule than any of them. At last, however,
the engine uttered three piercing blasts on its whistle, spat a
shower of hot coals from its smokestack, spewed a volcano
of live steam from its pistons, and began to snort alarmingly.

"Come on," yelled Eubie Buell, "she's agoing to light
out!" and dashed toward the car steps with all the
sightless determination of a head-down steer. Had not the
conductor stepped out upon the vestibule platform just in
time, he would have plunged completely over it, onto the
far-side tracks. But the trainman collided with him solidly,
straightened him around, and herded him into the car docile
as a muley cow. After that there was nothing to it. The
rest of the Comanches gave a whoop and charged the coach
as happily as though it were full of live Yankees firing back
at them.

It was still but three o'clock in the afternoon when they
took their seats. Five minutes later they were under way,
laughing and loud-talking as though they had ridden the
railroad all their lives. Buck, sided in his window seat by
faithful Miller Nalls, reviewed in his mind their situation,
as he watched the station slide away and the lovely spring
countryside appear to take its place. It seemed to him that
all was well. The sole problem at this point was Pablo
Massanet. The swamp boy, returned once more to Todo's
duffel sack, was stowed under the latter's seat and, depend-
ing on good luck and his ability to stand the pounding of

the wooden floor and the dust and cinders of the roadbed which came up through it, ought to ride to Vicksburg without discovery. There they could call a council and decide, finally, what to do about him. Buck, bone-weary, nodded to himself and settled in his seat. His mind at rest with his own, and his company's, behavior to this waypoint on their journey to the war, he was asleep within seconds. His next memory was that of Miller Nalls shaking him awake and of Miller's awed whisper in his ear.

"Buck! Buck, for Gawd's sake, lookit yonder!"

He shook his head, clearing the sleep haze, and peered out the window. Directly ahead, the roadbed made an S-bend to cross over a trestle. The timbers of the trestle were clearly visible from Buck's vantage, and the distance to them was not great for a prairie-trained eye. It was easy for Buck to see each detail of bracing and cross-bracing in the arched structure. And each eddy, current, and green backscum of the small stream beneath it. He could see, as well, each terrible line of the stark figure suspended between sun-bleached wood and brackish water, and his blue eyes widened and the sudden muffled beating of his heart came up high and sickeningly within him.

"Buck," breathed Miller, "it's him, ain't it?" Then, unbelievingly, "He said it, Buck. Jesus Gawd, he said they'd do it to him, and they done it! Buck, we ain't a mile out of town and they done it to him exactly like he said . . . !"

For the moment Buck could not speak.

The man under the bridge—the man hung dead by his neck from the center-span timber, his shoeless feet dragging the watercress and bank sand of the creek shallows—was the colored man who had begged Buck to let him go free so that he might run for his life; the colored man who was to be given a lecture and perhaps a lash or two by his loving owners when they got him home; the colored man who had looked out the window of the stagecoach and sung "Rock of Ages" softly to himself; the colored man who had known he was going to die and who had known how to do it.

Buck turned to Miller.

"Yes, Miller," he said, "they done it."

"I'll tell the boys," said Miller.

"No," Buck said, low-voiced, "don't do that. There's no need for them to know. We can't none of us help that poor man now."

Miller frowned, trying to understand. Buck put his hand on his knee and said quietly, "Miller, you want the boys to

suffer what you and me are suffering? You think they'll have
any answers for it we ain't got?"

"But, Buck, we kilt that darkie. We turnt him over to
them devils, and they strung him up."

"No, Miller," said Buck, "we didn't kill him, and I dassn't
think what did. Maybe I can figure it out, give time. Meanwhile, I don't want you to say nothing to the boys. That's
to spare *them,* Miller, not them devils back yonder. All right?"

"But, Buck . . ."

"Miller, it's an order."

The other boy looked at him peeringly and long. At last
he shook his head.

"If you say, Buck. You're the captain."

Buck looked over his shoulder, out the window. Behind
them the S-bend was disappearing in a stand of scrub pine
and shinnery oak. The trestle and the brackish creek were
gone. He turned again to Miller.

"It's better, Miller," he said, "believe me." Then, after a
troubled pause, "We've crossed over that bridge, let's forget
it if we can."

18   Vicksburg

THE MEMPHIS & NEW ORLEANS was the only trunkline
railroad west of the Mississippi. Its Louisiana spur, the
Vicksburg & Shreveport, was but a two-hour run from river
front to railhead. Thus it was still daylight when Buck and the
Comanches came in view of beautiful Vicksburg.

Seen from the Louisiana-side ferry-landing town of De
Soto, it was a sight to stun Far Western eyes. The famed bluffs
upon which the city stood rose three hundred feet above the
water. The effect, first seen at sunset, of the heights crowned
flamingo pink, the river and swamplands lying earth-brown
and leaf-green in the blue shadows of day's end, was breath-
taking. To buffalo grass boys prepared for it only by the
anemic experiences of Mendota and Shreveport, it seemed
a fairy city floating high above the ordinary flat world around
it. They could at first do nothing but gape in bumpkin awe at
its farflung, bluff-top splendor.

However, the ferryboat trip across the river gave them
time to recoup their confidence. Before their craft nosed
into the eastern levee, a company vote was taken to make of

Vicksburg what first Dallas, then Mendota, then Shreveport had failed to be. They had two hours to wait for their Vicksburg train to Montgomery, Alabama—next stop on the road to Richmond—and the thought that those hours might be spent in some far better way than sitting on the depot platform snatching flies, occurred as spontaneously as a rainbow breaking through August showers. Marching up the bluffs to the depot to get their tickets validated for the Montgomery Flyer, their yeasty spirits expanded with every step.

Miller Nalls, gazing about at the thronging clot of war-employed humanity, said to Buck, "What you thinking, Buck? You thinking the same as me?"

Buck, too, looked around before answering. "I'm thinking," he said at last, homely face lit with rare excitement, "that we're here; that, by God, Miller, we have made it! And that now, come what may, we will make it the rest of the way!"

"It's the same, Buck," murmured his slow-worded lieutenant. "The very same. Praise be."

"Yes, praise be," said Buck soberly, and led the way on up the bluff road to the city, and to the depot and marshaling yards of the Alabama & Vicksburg Railroad, where the Montgomery Flyer was making up for its night run through Mississippi.

Since the company had but five dollars to spend and six members to spend it, the matter of pocket money for doing the town might have been a problem. But, as captain, Buck gave first thought to his men. Foregoing his share, he rationed out one dollar each to Todo, Little Bit, Willy Bill, Miller and Eubie, directing them to squander it as they pleased. The sole condition was that they report back to the depot in one hour, at seven o'clock. This precaution was taken in view of the friendly warning given by the dispatcher that eight o'clock arrivals would find themselves bereft even of standing room on a military train going toward the front. Beyond this limitation the regrouping was left a matter of individual responsibility. Each man would carry his own ticket, serve as his own timepiece, Buck said. They then split up and disappeared, Todo with Little Bit, Willy Bill with Eubie. This left Buck, Miller and Pablo Massanet—very grateful to be out of his dusty berth in the duffel sack—to snatch flies, discuss the weather, spit at cracks, pitch pennies, or whatever.

Buck, taking the subject of his sermon from a pamphlet provided by the railroad, tried persuading Miller to take his dollar, go along uptown and see the square, the Warren County Courthouse, the statue of Reverend Newett Vick who had founded the city in 1808, and other things of intense interest to the intelligent visitor from Texas. But Miller balked. He did not want to go any place without Buck, he said, not even with a whole dollar to comfort him. Buck gave in, agreeing to accompany him, and with Pablo tagging along they set out for the center of the great city.

Once uptown, since neither Buck nor Miller were drinkers and Pablo couldn't afford to be, they decided to invest one-half of Miller's capital in a tourist guide. Their choice was a one-eyed, jersey-colored mulatto representing himself as a native son and college man who could prove the legitimacy of his business and professional status by the greasy hand-printed card in his hatband: "SEE ALL THE RIVER FORTS AND SHELLPROOFS 50¢. YOUR SATISFACTION ASSURED BY THE MANAGEMENT." This document impressed the Concho boys and although they had not originally had in mind a tour of the city's fortifications, their dusky dragoman proved such a convincing salesman that they were swept away. His theme was that if they were, as they claimed, officers in town with a troop of volunteer recruits, they owed it to their men to acquaint themselves with what they could of the military life, particularly fortifications.

"Now hold on there!" commanded Buck. "Let's just see fifty cents' worth of forts and let it go at that."

Their benefactor graciously took Miller's dollar, promising change upon conclusion of the tour, and set off to guide them down a rabbit warren of side streets and back allies. Ten minutes had passed. With them had passed their mulatto guide. One breath he was there, the next he had evaporated like a puff of powder smoke. Buck and Miller were left standing with Pablo on a darkening cribtown street corner waving figurative farewell to their dollar, their guide, and their fifty-cent tour of the famous river forts.

"Buck," said Miller, after a suitable silence, "I got an idea we've been took. What you think?"

"Miller," said Buck, looking around nervously, "I think you're reasonably close."

"Amigos," said Pablo Massanet, "I think you had better inquire for a new guide quick. This looks like a bad place."

"For sure," said Buck. "But who's going to lead us out of it?"

"I," answered Pablo. "And I will charge you nothing for the service."

"You mean," asked Buck, "that you actually know the way back out?"

"Where the Weasel goes, *Capitán,* the Weasel can come out. Follow me."

Lacking a better offer, Buck and Miller trailed sheepishly off after their small companion who, within a few minutes, had backtracked to the square, seeming to make every step a precise reverse of the rascally mulatto's. When Buck questioned him about this remarkable performance, he merely shrugged and tapped his head with one grubby forefinger.

"In here, *Capitán,*" he said, and that was all.

"I won't argue it," answered Buck. "Yonder's the depot and it's still only quarter to seven. Left to me, I'd have been down in them shanties till the war was over."

"You are too modest, *Capitán.* Of course you knew the way out. You were but testing me."

Miller looked at Buck with new respect.

"Is that the gospel, Buck?" he asked.

"Miller," said Buck, "shut up." Then, hurriedly. "See yonder. There's old Willy Bill and Eubie."

"Sure enough," said Miller, successfully decoyed. "You reckon they got took the same as us?"

"No, sir," said Buck, "not Eubie. He's the Weasel of Concho County. Likely they're just bored. Howdy, Willy Bill. Howdy, Eubie." They were up to their comrades now, but the latter did not respond to Buck's cheerful greeting. "What's ailing you two?" he demanded. "You look like something the cat would have drug in, but dassn't."

"Well," said Eubie, "you see there was this here feller had these three big paper-shell pecan hulls and this here little old dried-up goober pea . . ."

"Hold on," interrupted Buck, peering beyond the story-teller. "Ain't that Todo coming down the street?"

"Sure is," said Miller, "but he ain't got Tobin Earl with him. Damnation, that don't look good."

"It sure don't," muttered Buck. "Any time you separate them two you've did a day's work. Howdy, Todo. Where'd you lose your watch charm?"

Big Todo's face grew dark.

"'Bout a quarter-mile canter back yonder up Soldier Street," he answered. "He bet his dollar with some Alabama cavalrymen that he could drink a pint of whiskey standing on his head and not using his hands. Last I seen of him he had the bottle in his teeth and was heeling up agin the wall with his boots off." He paused, scowl deepening. "Then there was that cussed girl, too, and took all in all, I just up and told him to go to hell and I would see him up here when he had either strangled his idiot self, or the soldiers did it for him. But say, boys, that girl!" His broad face lighted to a positive glow. "She was really something! You know, she was why old Tobin Earl was atrying to run his dollar into a decent stake. He'd talked price to her and found out she wanted three dollars Federal."

"Todo," said Buck sternly, "where is the damn fool?"

"Like I told you. Quarter mile up Soldier Street. That's the gaudy one yonder. Starts past them sided boxcars. See where all them lights is turning on?"

"You oughtn't to have left him alone," said Buck.

"Well, hell, I'm not his mother. You go get him. You're the captain."

"That's so," admitted Buck, "and I will do it. You all stay here. What did you say the name of the saloon was, Todo?"

"Name? Hell, I dunno. Never stopped long enough to look. It's the one with the pink flamingos and purple wall paint out front. And with the big darkey standing in the street dressed like one of them A-rab sheiks or turkey trot sultans. He's abowing and awaving a lit torch. And grinning and gabbing you right on into where the women and whiskey is at. You take a good gander at that red-headed filly, Buck. The one Little Bit is aiming to saddle. Oh, my, I will tell you she would melt the bluing right off your gunbarrel, man!"

"Hush up," ordered Buck, and swung away stiff-shouldered and scowlingly.

19 Battle of
South Levee Street

HE TOOK PABLO MASSANET with him for the reason that when he got into Soldier Street and looked around, after expressly telling Pablo to stay with the others, there at his heels was his faithful shadow. Having no time to take the boy back, he snapped at him to follow along, upon pain of dismissal from the Comanches if he disobeyed once more. The rest happened so swiftly Buck had no trustful recollection of it.

There was no difficulty separating the Arabian Nights from the other tawdry soldier-traps strung like cheap oriental pearls along the street Todo had called "Soldier" but which Buck noted was marked South Levee Street. Even fifty paces away Buck could hear the uproar going on within the bistro and could tell from its animal sound that someone was getting hurt inside. Knowing Tobin Earl Luckett's propensity for putting his mouth where his money was not, he spoke tersely to Pablo.

"*Hombre,* stand guard. I'm going inside. I don't come back out in five minutes, you go fetch the Comanches." He held up, listening to the growing furor. "Better make that three minutes," he added. "Or two."

"*Si, Capitán.* I will count to one hundred by tens and then run."

"That's better yet," grinned Buck, and ran past the giant Negro doorman into the South Levee Street saloon.

Once inside, the situation did not seem so formidable. It was only a very ordinary fight going on—one civilian backed against the bar fending off three soldiers—and it sounded so bad only because the place was jammed with people shouting on the battlers. The only factor which alarmed Buck was the identity of the lone civilian.

"Hold on, Little Bit!" he yelled. "The Comanches are coming!"

Buck Burnet, quiet and unassuming as was his ordinary manner, did not come by his red hair dishonestly. Buck would walk five miles to go around a bad fight, or crawl ten miles to get into a good one. The three Alabama cavalrymen were on their backsides before they realized there was another man in the melee.

"Beat it," laughed Buck to Little Bit. "I can handle these pistolnecks with one hand. Go get the boys and we will clean out the whole Alabama Horse Artillery!"

But the boast was ill-advised and the enemy had reinforcements much nearer than the Alabama & Vicksburg railway depot. The next moment no less than a dozen Confederate regulars were charging the bar and Buck and Little Bit were forced to grab bottles and begin backing for the door. On the way Buck took time to gasp out the question as to what had started the fight. Little Bit, busy as he was, took pause between swings of the poker-table chairs with which they had now armed themselves, to explain that, consistent with history, it had been a woman.

"That scrawny one yonder!" he shouted, felling a member

of the Tuscaloosa Light Rifles who had just enlisted with the
1st Alabama Cavalry. "The one with the swampcat eyes and
varmint teeth!"

"You mean that off-color redhead?" panted Buck, evading
a flung gin bottle and taking a cavalry boot in the solar
plexus for his dexterity. "The one ducking down the bar?"

"That's the one," grinned Little Bit through an upper lip
split nearly to the nostril. "Faithful type. Man, lookit her
sprint for that back door. You couldn't catch her with a
cutting pony. Not unless she looked around and seen you
wave three dollars."

"Don't talk," groaned Buck, going to his knees from a
tremendous blow, "fight . . .!"

Fight they did, then, both of them. And like Concho
County bobcats. But their best was only good enough to
get them to the door and into the street. There they were
forced into a flank retreat along the gaudy front of the
Arabian Nights to a noisome side alley where, their backs
to a stack of refuse barrels, garbage buckets and empty
whiskey cases, they took their last stand.

Having seen, in wheeling for the flank maneuver, that
Pablo had deserted his post, Buck spat a piece of broken
tooth into the dust and informed Little Bit that if he did
not at once break off the engagement and get up to the depot
to fetch the Comanches, they would never make it to Richmond. Little Bit was reluctant to abandon the field but
Buck made it an order and, in a lull occasioned by Buck
dropping three of the enemy with a single overhead crash
of an emptied tap-beer barrel, he turned and fled down the
alley. As he did, the Alabamans regrouped to close on Buck
with a ringing Rebel yell, and that was Buck's last conscious
memory of the Battle of South Levee Street.

20   The Prostitute

BUCK'S SENSES RETURNED SLOWLY. At first he wondered idly
if he had died and if this might be the hereafter. It
was a room, he decided. Then, after further squinting study,
he could see that it was in no way celestial but very human
indeed. Its centerpiece was the antiquated iron bed upon

which, shirtless and bootless, he lay. It was small, dark, clutteringly furnished, past all question a woman's room. There was the cheap gilt mirror over the harp-legged New Orleans dressing table. The plaster statuette of the Saviour on its shabby bracket over the bed. The faded cromo of madonna and child hung awry on the far wall. The oval-backed boudoir chair with tapestried seat worn threadbare. The chipped water pitcher and granite basin on the washstand. The corner wardrobe-pole with its sad fringy line of party-hall dresses. The yellowed lace curtains at the single casement window. The half dozen week-old roses in the ruby glass vase. And then, lastly, there was the woman herself. Not woman really, either, thought Buck, but child. Yet child old as sin was old. And lovely as evil is always lovely. He gazed up at her, plundered alike of breath and speech.

She was not beautiful. Her mouth was too wide, her skin too dark, her cheekbones too prominent, her entire expression too clearly foreign. Yet Buck could not remove his eyes from her. She leaned over him, then, and he tasted her breath upon his lips as though it were a quick, softly blown kiss.

"How do you feel?" she asked. "Are you all right?"

The voice matched the face, feral, low-toned, disturbingly familiar, and Buck's puzzlement grew in pace with his uneasiness.

"I think I'm all right, thank you," he said, sitting up and swinging his legs over the side of the bed. "If you please, miss, where's my shirt?"

"It hasn't dried. The blood on it was quite bad. I have washed it for you."

Buck's mind was clearing rapidly. He glanced again around the room. "Miss, how did I get here? It's your place, ain't it?"

"Yes, it's my place. I had you carried here."

"You did? Whatever for?"

The girl dropped her eyes. "I don't know, I just wanted to help you."

Buck's memories of the fight came back. He shook his head. "Why me? You surely weren't helping my friend any."

"I didn't care about him."

"Then why on earth would you care about me?"

The girl searched his face before answering, looking for a sign that he might be feeling some of the same things she was feeling. But he was not and she replied with simple honesty. "I cannot say. Just because it was you, I think."

Buck nodded, stood up painfully. "Well, miss, I am beholden to you, regardless. You saved me from a terrible
beating, maybe worse."

"Worse, I believe. I have seen many such fights."

Buck studied her. There was still something about her
which kept digging at his memory. Something in the intent
brilliance of her eyes, the slim quickness of her movements
the oddly dignified, almost foreign way in which she phrased
her words. But whatever it was it would not fall into meaning-
ful place.

"How did you do it, miss? Stop the fight, I mean," he
asked. "There must have been a dozen of them and you
don't weigh no more than a sack of shelled corn."

The girl looked at him with a smile which flickered and
was gone like heat lightning.

"When you saw me run away," she said, "I was not running
away; I was running to bring the Provost Marshal's men, the
soldier police."

A shadow of concern crossed Buck's face. "Seems to me,"
he said, "that running to bring the military law down on
soldiers would be bad for business at a place like the Arabian
Nights. I sort of got the idea you worked there."

"I did," replied the girl.

"You lost your job over me?" said Buck, frowning.

"I can get another," she shrugged. "For a girl like me
there is always work."

Buck spoke quickly, without thinking. "Yes, I suppose
so. What kind of work do you do, miss?"

Instantly, he knew he had been a fool. And, worse than
that, unkind. When the girl stared at him, dark face flushed
with embarrassment—no, deep shame—Buck knew what
her reply was going to be. Indeed, what it had to be. She
was a girl no older than he but in a business considerably
older than both of them. Belatedly, he sought to soften his
cruelty.

"I mean," he began, "that—well, uh, you don't seem to
be . . ." He broke off, then blurted desperately, "I mean
what's a nice girl like you doing in a place like that?"

She looked at him a moment, then said very humbly,
" 'A nice girl.' That's a very strange and kind thing for you
to say."

Buck was not conscious of the tears brimming her eyes,
nor did he see her reach to take his hand. It was only when
she murmured, *"Con su permiso, señor,"* and pressed the
hand to her lips that he seized it away from her and cried
out, "Here! you can't do that. It ain't fitting."

She looked at him another long moment, then placed her hands on his bare shoulders. "I cannot help the way I feel," she said, "and you are the first man in four years to call me a nice girl. Do you think I can forget that? Or forget you for saying it?"

Buck stiffened and drew away, every instinct tensing him to run. "Lady," he told her. "I got to get my shirt and get out of here!" But she only moved forward again, bringing the warmth of her body into his. Her parted lips glistened in the half-darkness, calling him down to them in a language understood beyond any strictures of innocence.

"Do you?" was all she said.

He lay on the bed with the girl, not knowing if she slept, or if she were awake and waiting for him to say the first word. It was cooling in the little room now. High above the shabby rooftops visible through the casement window, the sky was still touched with the last of the day's light. But in the street below, the oil lamps had been lit and the gray of twilight was blurring the scarcely covered figures of the street women as they came out to sit upon the worn stone steps of their hovels and to rest in the first fresh breath of evening against the humid chores of the night to come.

The girl had been surpassingly wonderful, Buck thought. He did not care who she was or what she might be. She was made for Buck and he was made for her. From this hour of this night the whole world had changed for Buck Burnet.

He was careful not to awaken the girl in coming off the bed to a barefoot stand by the tapestried chair which held his clothing. Quickly he dressed, quickly turned to quit the room. Yet he could not do it, could not bring himself to creep away like a sneakthief in the night, leaving her to guess where he had gone, and why, and if she might ever see him again.

A token, he thought; he must leave for her some kind of a token. But what? A hasty search of his pockets yielded nothing. Anxiously he scanned the room. The roses in the vase? The roses placed in some way beneath the Saviour to say that he loved her and would always love her? But could he be sure she would know that he meant that? His hand went to his chin, big fingers worrying the red stubble. In the movement his wrist brushed his chest, striking the golden locket which he wore there in secret. Only Miller Nalls, of all the Comanches, knew he had it, hidden there beneath his ranch boy's high-necked undershirt. It was his mother's, the only thing of hers which had come down to

Buck. The whole of his heritage from the parents he had
been too tiny to remember the night the Kwahadis came.
And the night the Rangers came too late behind them. The
locket, then, was literally all Buck could give the girl. The
locket and the timeless three-word message graved upon its
inner face.

Tenderly he arranged the offering, posing the chain so
that when the girl touched the flowers she must find the
locket. When he had finished, he wanted to look at her for
a last time but dared not. Swiftly, stealthily, he went out of
the room and down the narrow hallway leading to the street
door below. There, as his hand hesitated above the latch,
he was startled by a sudden pounding upon the outer panels
and a high voice crying out stridently, "Open up! It is
useless for you to deny that you hold *El Capitán* prisoner
in there. If you do not immediately release him into my
custody, I shall order my men to the attack!"

Buck flung the door wide. Seizing his would-be rescuer,
he pleaded fervently, "Lord A'mighty, Pablo, simmer down!
You want them army police storming back up the street?"
But before the swamp boy could reply, a low cry arose out
of the darkness and the girl appeared in the doorway behind
Buck. "Pablo?" she said. "Can it be possible? Our own small
Pablo!"

" 'Our own small Pablo'?" said the boy, alarmed and
backing away. *"Cuidado, Capitán!* She has been drinking."
Then, eyeing Buck doubtfully, "Is this the one for whom you
have had your head cracked open? This thin, scrawny thing
with the voice like a molting gray heron? *Quita!* God forbid!"

"Pablito!" the girl exclaimed, laughing. "It *is* you! The
same mean small animal as ever. Here, let me see you. Come.
Stand in a better light. Yes, yes, it is you, my own dear
little brother. *Qué tal, qué tal . . ."*

"Little brother?" echoed Buck. "Him? Yours? It can't
be. It ain't humanly possible."

"Capitán," apologized Pablo, peering from the protection of
Buck's backside, "I am afraid that it is. I cannot see the
face too well in this poor light but I am remembering the
voice with a shudder. Eh, say there, skinny girl, are you truly
my sister? Be careful what you say, I have a way of knowing
if you lie, a question you must answer just so. Listen now.
What is the name of the small animal by which the mother
calls me?"

"Comedreja!" cried the girl. "The Weasel!"

"Ay de mí!" sighed Pablo to Buck. "I am sorry, *Capitán,*
but it appears as though you have found my sister. But she

will fatten with good care, I swear it! Do not judge her too hastily. You would not buy a sack of beans in this light, *Capitán*. Besides, she is . . ."

"Pablo," said Buck, "be quiet. I've got to think."

"But there is no time to think, *Capitán*. That is what I came to tell you." Pablo made a quick move to avoid the girl, who had put out her hand to touch him. "Keep away from me, sister," he warned. "I am a man now." Then swiftly back to Buck. "The train, *Capitán*, it is leaving in five minutes."

"Five minutes!" exclaimed Buck. "What time *is* it?"

"Who cares what time it is?" demanded Pablo. "Five minutes is five minutes. What does it matter which hour it is taken from? Are you coming, *Capitán*, or must we depart without you?"

Buck, listening to the boy, was taken with one of the genuine inspirations of his life. He had given his word as a Burnet to do what he might toward persuading Pablo's sister to go home if he should meet her upon the road to war. Now, miraculously, he *had* come upon her and his word must be redeemed. And the redeeming, happily, would serve the double purpose of discharging Pablo Massanet from active service with the Concho County Comanches. It would, that is, if he could get the girl to agree to go home, and the boy to agree to go with her. That, indeed, was his inspiration.

When he spoke to them of it he was pleasantly surprised. Despite his small brother's bravado, Pablo was impressed with his slim sister. The idea of taking on the grown man's job of chaperoning her on the trip back to the Caddo home place seemed to strike just the right chord of family loyalty within him. Buck was delighted. If the swamp boy's compliance was too ready, he did not appear to note it. Or, noting it, made nothing of it. The matter was settled with a handshake between him and Pablo, a fumbling, brief embrace between him and Pablo's sister. It was only when he turned to go, saying, "*Adiós*, Pablo; *adiós* . . ." that he realized he didn't even know the girl's name. As he paused guiltily, she supplied it with a laugh.

"Gaby," she told him. "For Gabrielle." Then with a gay little wave and the first real pride he had heard in her, "For Gabrielle Marie Celeste Massanet!"

Returning the gesture with his homely freckled grin, he made a self-conscious play at saluting her.

"Buck, ma'am," he said. "For William Buckley Burleson Burnet!" Then, softly, and with no smile, "Wait for me Gaby. Wait—and pray."

21 The Fatal Halt
at Marion Junction

BUCK REACHED THE DEPOT and joined the others aboard the Flyer with twenty seconds to spare. It was then discovered that Little Bit Luckett had misplaced his ticket. The overworked conductor, not even pausing to consider excuses, picked up the startled youth and dropped him bodily over the vestibule railing to the platform planking below. Buck was required to jump off the train, pick up, dust, and return with the fallen Little Bit. Meanwhile, Todo MacLean had put his brawny fists under the conductor's lapels, raised him eighteen inches in the air, and talked to him soberingly. In wise result, the trainman agreed that Little Bit might ride on trust to the next station. At this, Todo put him back down upon the floor and Eubie Buell took out of his midsection the muzzle of his old Walker Colt, which he had placed there merely as a precaution against Todo losing his grip on the lapels. The conductor made good his escape up the car aisle, but Buck's evening was only beginning.

The next disturbance came when, with the train gathering speed past the Vicksburg way points of Hall's Ferry Road, Clay Street, Railroad Redoubt and Confederate Avenue, his restless gaze wandered across the aisle to fall upon a familiar duffel sack wedged beneath big Todo's seat. Indicating the sack and staring down its guilty-looking guardian, Buck demanded sharply, "What's that damned thing doing here?" and Todo put out his jaw and said, "Well, damn it to hell, Buck, the Weasel still ain't got a ticket!" and the latter popped his beady-eyed head out of the sack and squeaked, *"Si, Capitán,* that is so," and Buck was surrounded again.

He could not, of course, allow the insubordination.

Going forward in the car, he inquired politely of the conductor as to the first stop ahead.

"Cumpston's Corners, fifteen miles," replied the other suspiciously. "Why for you want to know?"

"Thank you, sir," said Buck. "I wish you would just tell me when we are there."

He then returned to the Comanches and held a quiet talk

80

with them, making it very clear they were embarked upon the last leg of their hard journey and that the business of Pablo Massanet had to be disposed of with no further foolishness. They must realize, he told them, that in their frontline future there could be no safe place for a thirteen-year-old youth. Montgomery lay ahead, and then Richmond. They might well hear the roar of enemy artillery before the week was out. Did they want to share that fearsome sound with a small boy? The only son of aging parents? Or did they not agree with Buck that the lad must be put off the train at the next station, and ordered to return to his grieving father and mother?

Naturally, the Comanches could see it then. The Weasel had been a lot of fun but none of them wanted to see him hurt. As well, all of them had good memories of his folks. They now realized, and admitted honestly, that they should not have conspired to get him aboard the stage from Shreveport, much less having joined in sneaking him onto the cars out of Vicksburg. From here on, they vowed, they would back Buck and no more nonsense. With the matter thus settled, there remained only the difficult task of conveying the decision to Pablo Massanet. As was his place, Buck shouldered that responsibility.

At Cumpston's Corners he carried the duffel sack off the train and out of sight behind a rickety telegrapher's shack crouched at trackside. Here he opened the sack and commanded the boy to crawl out and come to attention.

"Pablo," he began solemnly, "this here thing of being a soldier ain't always so simple. I got now to tell you something which is going to take some standing up to."

"*Si, Capitán,*" shrugged the boy. "I am standing." Buck shook his head. "It ain't what I mean, Pablo. A soldier comes in all shapes and sizes. Now your size ain't exactly—no, hell, it ain't your size that's wrong either."

"What is it, then, that *is* wrong?" asked Pablo anxiously.

"You got to go home," said Buck. "You got to get off the train and go home."

"I am already off the train, *Capitán,*" said the boy, eyeing him with a hurt-dog look. "That is easy for one of your size to do to one of my size." His small chin came up defiantly. "But how will you make me go home?"

"I won't make you go," said Buck. "You'll make yourself go."

"Are you crazy, *Capitán?* I leave the war and go home, of my own order? Never! I am a Massanet."

"So is your sister a Massanet," said Buck quietly.

"My sister? Bah! She is a woman, she can take care of herself."

"Pablo," said Buck, "answer me one question. Do you remember what I called you when I first came to your home in the *brasada?* When I needed help for the boy with the sick leg?"

"Si, Capitán. You called me a little bastard."

Buck flushed. "No," he said. "I mean after that."

"After that," replied the boy proudly, "you called me *'hombre,'* a man."

"Exactly so," said Buck. "Now then, what would be the first duty of a man to his lost sister? And to his grieving old parents? Them as had no other son? Them which had prayed so hard in their lonesome hearts for the return of this here same lost sister?"

"Please, *Capitán,* this is not an equal thing. I cannot fight your words."

"It's your own words you can't fight, Pablo," Buck said tersely. "You gave me your promise you would see your sister safe home. We shook hands on it." He paused, as the engine's whistle blasted a shrill warning. "Now you will either stand to your oath, or you won't," he concluded. "It's for you to say, *hombre.*"

The swamp boy straightened. The effort brought the top of his shaggy head very nearly to Buck's beltline.

"I am a Massanet, *Capitán,*" he said. "I will look to the girl, as agreed. *Adiós.*"

"No," said Buck, offering his hand, "not *adiós. Hasta luego.*"

"As you will, *Capitán. Hasta luego* then, but no more handshakes. If we are soldiers, let us part like soldiers."

He stepped back, saluting with ramrod stiffness. Buck returned the salute smartly. Pablo Massanet wheeled by the right flank, marched off into the early spring darkness. In the sudden, covering noise of the engine's pistons spurting steam and its sanded drive wheels biting into the track iron behind him, Buck could not be certain of the final thing he heard from the direction of the proudly departed, littlest soldier of the Concho County Comanches. But it sounded to him very much like a small boy sobbing.

Following the balky start from Vicksburg and the painful delay at Cumpston's Corners, things went very smoothly aboard the cars until about three o'clock in the morning, when the Alabama-bound Flyer slowed joltingly hard for the crossing of its tracks with those of the northward running Mobile & Ohio at Marion Junction, just outside Marion, Mississippi.

From the junction crossing the M & O went up through Macon and Tupelo to Corinth and the Tennessee border, one hundred ninety miles away. At the moment a troop train from Florida with the last of General Braxton Bragg's army corps of ten thousand men was stalled across the Alabama & Vicksburg's line. The reason for the delay was a fateful one for Buck Burnet and his five friends.

Thirty head of cavalry remounts had broken loose from stock cars on the M & O and were running free. They were half-wild western range ponies from Matamoros, Texas. The moment the Concho County boys, leaning out their windows, saw the wiry mustangs from home they leaped for the vestibule exit.

Outside, the moonlight was bright as day. It shone on a scene of typical military brilliance. The cursing soldiers detailed to guard the stock cars—naturally city boys from the Eastern seaboard—were helpless to capture the frightened range horses. By some oversight of assignment, however, the hard-bitten Alabama sergeant in charge of the detail *was* a veteran horseman. Moreover, he had worked in Texas prior to the war. When he saw the bow-legged Concho volunteers coming up from the stalled Montgomery Flyer, he at once ordered his urban troopers to stand aside and give the country boys room to swing their loops. His faith was well guided.

Miller Nalls had brought on his braided rawhide *reata* from Shreveport. Now, throwing the snaking, underhand loop, which could forefoot or heel a running horse from forty feet, and trading off on the roping with Buck and Eubie Buell while the others hazed and tied, he had the mustangs standing quietly on picket in less than half an hour—an altogether remarkable performance even for a West Texan aided by West Texans.

But Fate was not through with Miller Nalls and the Concho County Comanches. The Confederate colonel in command of the pick-up regiment aboard the M & O, hence responsible for the delivery of the remounts to martinet Bragg, had walked back along the train in time to witness the last few head being caught and brought to hand. Now he stood beside his tough Alabama sergeant nodding thoughtfully to himself.

"Yes, sir," he said. Then, emphatically, "Yes indeed, sir!" Turning to the sergeant, he added pleasantly, "Barnes, will you kindly bring those men to my car when you are able?"

The sergeant went over to Buck and thanked him and the others, freely admitting he had never seen anything to equal their handling of the horses. As quickly, he became curt, stiffening his back along with his voice.

"All right, boys," he ordered. "Line up and follow me."

"Hold on," said Buck suspiciously. "Follow you for what?"

"For to see the Colonel."

"What colonel?" asked Buck, eyeing him.

"Colonel Boykin."

"What's he colonel of?"

"The Pensacola Light Blues. That's us."

"Oh," said Buck politely. "You Florida boys?"

"Nope, just stationed there."

"Where you going?"

"To take you to the colonel, happen you will shut up and follow along."

"Supposing we don't?"

"Colonel said to bring you."

"What's that mean?"

"Means we'll bring you."

The hard-faced sergeant made a signal with his hand, and his squad of troopers took a threatening step forward. Buck considered the odds. There were six of his Comanches armed with a rawhide rope, a sawed-off shotgun, assorted sheath knives and a hogleg pistol or two. Against that were eight trained Southern soldiers each carrying a loaded Long Tom Mississippi Rifle. The leader of the Concho County corps decided to retreat with caution.

"Well, now, my good fellow," he said airily to the sergeant, "I do believe we are keeping you from your regular work. If you will be so kind as to point out the general location of Colonel Boykin's car, I am certain sure we can find our way to it without putting you to further bother."

"Oh, my," announced the other witheringly, "I do predict a grand future for you in this man's army, lad. You will find the regular C.S.A. just the place for a jolly wit and nimble tongue."

"Why, thank you," beamed Buck. "I am right pleased to learn that, for my friends and me are bound for Richmond to enlist in the cause of our country."

"Is that so?" said the Confederate veteran. "Well, I do believe that if you will follow me I can save you several miles in that ambition."

"How is that?" asked Buck carefully.

"Why, that is like this," responded the sergeant, leading the way up the track. "You see we got quite a nice little war of our own agoing just over the line in Tennessee. Morever, this here very train we are on is bound for there, this minute."

"See here," challenged Buck, genuinely alarmed now. "What has that got to do with us? We got a train of our own and tickets on it paid clean through to Virginia. We ain't interested in going no other place."

"You will like Tennessee in April," said the cynical Alabama sergeant. "There ain't a prettier piece of country in the whole South than that stretch up there around Shiloh Church, acrost the line from Corinth."

"What church?" asked Buck Burnet.

"Shiloh," answered the older man indifferently. The Texas boy nodded, relieved, and followed along after him and thought no more of it than that it was a lovely, soft sort of name and ought, by rights, to go with a tolerably pretty kind of country.

22 Assignment in Corinth

THE DELAYED Mobile & Ohio troop train left Marion Junction crossing at 4:00 A.M., April 3. Aboard the short string of coaches and stock cars were thirty horses and three hundred sixty-eight men of the Pensacola Light Blues, attached to Bragg's corps. Among the illy trained number were six West Texas volunteers who had been sworn summarily into Albert Sidney Johnston's ragtag Army of the Mississippi. Inside a single hour their simple frontier conception of the war had been destroyed. It was presently being rebuilt along more realistic, if less agreeable, lines.

"Well," shrugged Mercer Barnes, the deliberate Alabama sergeant, "what did I tell you boys?" He looked around at the glum Comanches, nodding paternally. "I vow you would need to have gone another eight hundred miles to find a fight to touch the one we will find for you up yonder in Tennessee."

"Yes," added his moon-faced corporal, Tellis Yeager, a Georgia plowboy. "Let me tell you, you are sure lucky to have fell afoul of old Mercer and me."

"You," continued Sergeant Barnes, "are going to make out in the army as well as your friend Red, yonder." He hooked a thumb at Buck. "At least you are if you stay in the infantry."

"Which we ain't going to do," countered Eubie. "We are born cavalry and will not fight afoot."

"You will fight," nodded the sergeant, "when and where and how you are told." He had suddenly lost his easy air. "You boys don't seem to savvy the fact you've been legally swore into the C.S.A. Ain't you any rightful idea what that article of enlistment means? Wasn't you listening when the adjutant read it for you?"

"We was listening," Buck put in dispiritedly, "but you're right we didn't savvy what we heard."

"Well," said the sergeant, not unkindly, "maybe I can lay it out for you a little plainer. You was grabbed where the hair was short and you're going to have it harder than you got any notion of."

He paused, eyeing them a moment. Buck took the opportunity to say, "Yes, and that's just the part we don't savvy. Why was *we* grabbed? Just poor ranch boys from way out West? What good *we* going to do this here General Bragg? I thought you said he had near onto ten thousand men. What's he want of six more?"

Mercer Barnes held up his hand. "If you will hush up, boy," he said, "I will try to tell you."

"Yes, sir," said Buck.

"Now, then," Barnes began, "you got to remember that Bragg's ten thousand is only a part of Johnston's army. Besides Bragg, we got old Bishop Polk with two divisions from up in Tennessee, General Hardee with his Bluegrass boys, John Breckinridge with three brigades of good Western mountain rifles, a Kentucky cavalry outfit under John Hunt Morgan, a whole damned regiment of volunteer horse under Nathan Bedford Forrest, and, if them names don't rouse you, try General P.G.T. Beauregard, hisself! Yes, sir, that's right, Old Borry's second in command to Johnston. Nor even that ain't all. Across the river we got General Earl Van Dorn coming down from Arkansas with his and Price's and McCulloch's Missouri lads what fought so grand at Pea Ridge. Boys, I tell you, one way or another we got forty thousand men on the ground right now, with another ten or twelve thousand due overnight!"

He paused, caught up in his own excitement, then swept on.

"Against that, across the line up there in Tennessee around Shiloh Church where I said, there's only that new feller, Grant, and maybe thirty-five thousand Yanks. With Grant you got a flock of second-rate chicken-gutters like Prentiss, McClernand, Lew Wallace and that there feller they call 'Crazy' Sherman. It ain't much of a command you can bet. And our scouts say they ain't showing the haziest signs they know there's a Confederate army any closer to them than the garrison at Vicksburg. Now I wouldn't ask you, ordinary, to swallow all this. But I got it right straight off'n General Bragg's staff sergeant, and if Bragg don't know what's going on, *nobody* in this man's army does.

"This here sergeant told me the Federals was spread around like a Baptist camp meeting, strung out all the way from Nine Mile Island to Pittsburg Landing. If that's so, boys, I will guarantee you they're as good as hung up and throat-cut right now. All we got to do is go in and stick them. It's a certain chance, Bragg says, for the biggest Confederate sweep since Manassas. He claims Johnston could end the whole damned war day after tomorrow. Now how do you like them reasons and resolutions, Red?"

Buck shook his head, bewildered.

"Why, I like them fine, I reckon," he said. "But I don't see where they add up to us six boys getting took off our train to Richmond and shoved onto this here one for Corinth. How come it to be us? We surely wasn't the onliest ones they could have grabbed off them Richmond cars."

"That's right," said Barnes. "But you sure as hell was the onliest ones which jumped off them cars and come running to round up old Bragg's remount."

"Yes," amplified owl-eyed Corporal Tellis Yeager. "And got yourselves see'd doing it by Colonel Boykin."

"How's that?" said Buck.

"Like this," answered Barnes sharply. "Bragg needs them horses vital bad. When you all took after and tied down them damned broomtails, you just plain elected yourselves to get sent into action along with them. Now that's a certain fact, boys, and you can write home about it."

"You mean," cried Buck, "that we're going to get the chance to do some scouting for General Bragg up there to Shiloh Church?"

"I mean," said Barnes, "that you will get the chance to do some shoveling for him."

"Shoveling?"

"Yes, sir. The only scouting you will be doing for the General is for fresh horse apples along his staff picket line."

"You're joshing," said Buck, white-lipped.

"Oh no, I ain't," denied Barnes. "That's what you'll be doing, Colonel Boykin's orders. You and the dumb-faced feller and the wiseacre towhead." He confirmed the last two identifications with finger stabs at Miller and Eubie. "The three of you been assigned to go along with these here mustangs to old Bragg."

He bobbed his head. "Like I told you, Red," he said, "you'll have a grand time in Tennessee."

The train came into Corinth at 10:00 A.M. The town was unnaturally still and empty. There were scarcely any soldiers at the depot, none at all on the deserted streets. The Texas boys looked at one another. From what they had been told on the ride up, they had expected to see Albert Sidney Johnston sitting his horse waiting for their train to pull in. And they had figured to hear, rolling over the ridges and through the valleys beyond the town, the roar of cannon and the rattle of rifle fire. Instead it was so quiet in Corinth they could hear a horsefly buzz a boxcar length away.

It was an illusion, lasting only as long as it took Mercer Barnes to scout the depot stragglers. He was back in five minutes. And there was news. General Johnston was at his command post outside town. A general staff meeting had been called for 11:00 A.M. The rumored reason for the meeting was man-sized: the Army of the Mississippi was to advance north at twelve noon.

As Buck and the Comanches climbed down from their car bug-eyed over this information, Barnes dashed off again, this time toward the head of the train and Colonel Boykin's car. Once more his return was swift.

"Get them horses off the cars," he directed, "and walk them out to where they will lead quiet up to old Bragg's camp. Colonel says you'll have to hop it, as he wants to see Bragg before the staff meeting. Truth is, he dassn't hold up those nags one minute."

"That Bragg must be a real old catamount," said Willy Bill sociably.

"Sonny," Barnes assured him, "you ain't seen a catamount yet. Bragg's a ring-tailed ape. He will drill you to death six days a week and wind you up with a ten-mile hike for Sunday fun." He paused, weighing it fairly. "I reckon you could say he's a total son of a bitch and never get sued for slander. For a fact, he is the most hated general officer in the Confederate States Army. There simply ain't nobody that likes old Bragg."

"How about Mrs. Bragg?" asked Willy Bill.

Barnes studied him. "That's three," he finally said.

"Three what?" said Willy Bill.

"Three of you Alamo heroes what are going to be big successes in the Army. Don't they raise nothing but smart alecs in Texas?"

"I don't know," said Willy Bill. "I ain't seen all of Texas."

"I'll keep you in mind," promised Mercer Barnes, and turned to Buck. "Red," he said, "get them horses lined up to go. Bragg's waiting."

Half an hour later Colonel Boykin led the thirty Texas mustangs toward General Braxton Bragg's tent. They went mincingly and well mannered as so many Tennessee plantation ponies. With them, to keep them that way, marched the six-man squad of the Concho County Comanches, Buck Burnet still in nominal command. But the orderly passage of the nervous Western horses and their buckskin-shirted escorts was nonetheless novelty enough to raise a highly audible stir. Bragg, hearing it, was already outside his tent fuming with impatience when Boykin, calm as cold soup, brought the cavalcade to a halt. While the colonel of the Light Blues presented his report, Buck covertly examined the dreaded commander of the Florida Corps.

To begin with, Bragg could be called "old" only by a very young man, or by one who used the word to describe somebody of any age. Buck estimated him to be late fortying but so fiercely intent as to appear more than that. His very dark eyes gleamed like live coals. Buried deep in his head, they seemed to move constantly, reminding Buck of the eyes of a stoat or ferret. He was full bearded, both hair and whiskers black as stove polish except where the silver had touched the temples. Add to this, Buck thought, a long hook nose, jug-handle ears, low forehead, jutting craggy brows and a short, monkey-strong body, long-armed and bent-legged and nervously strung up as the rest of him, and you had yourself a pretty fair field sketch of General Braxton Bragg at Corinth, Mississippi, April 3, 1862.

Buck and the Comanches could not hear the exchange between Bragg and Boykin, but almost at once Bragg was waving to Buck and shouting, "Come on, come on! Bring up the horses, on the double! We shan't be here all spring!" and Buck was left to judge that along with his other virtues Bragg was disinclined toward patience.

It developed, however, that he was pleased with the new horses. It was the first and last time Buck saw him in that condition about anything. Boykin, the easygoing, nonprofessional Confederate officer, the archetype of his kind in the Southern Army—the kind who was always first concerned

with the welfare of his troops and only then worried about
losing the war to the Union—now began to embellish for
Bragg the story of the remount capture by the Texas boys.
He had got as far as his subsequent spot enlistment of the
latter when Bragg broke loose.

"I am not interested, Colonel," he snarled, "in your im-
pressions, but only in the matter of having these remounts
delivered. I shall inquire later into your having allowed
them to delay you. Texas boys, eh . . . ?" His black eyes
pounced on Buck. "You!" he stabbed. "Step up here!"

Buck moved out quickly enough but forgot to salute and
stand braced.

"Attention!" rasped Bragg.

"Yes, sir," smiled Buck, still not bracing.

"Straighten up, you damn fool!" hissed Eubie Buell.

Bragg wheeled about and barked, "Who said that?"

"I did, General," said Eubie. "You see, General, old Buck
he don't understand all about soldiering, just yet."

"And you do?" inquired Bragg politely.

"Oh, sure."

"Then, sir, you will understand that if you utter another
word I shall have you flogged."

"Yes *sir*," said Eubie, and froze stiff as Lot's wife.

"Now, then," Bragg said to Buck, "when an officer ad-
dresses you, or you address an officer, you will salute and
stand properly to attention. Is that clear?"

"As mountain spring water, General."

"And you will not add any qualifications. You will simply
reply 'yes sir' or 'no sir.' Do I make myself abundantly
plain?"

"Yes, sir," began Buck, "plain as the pimple on the end
of your . . ." He caught himself. "Yes, sir," he said.

Bragg gave him a flicking head-bob for the effort, and
proceeded to question him keenly about the horses. It was
then Buck saw a little of what lay behind that angry ex-
terior. Bragg learned more about horses in ten minutes than
most men learn in a lifetime. Buck felt he was lucky to
survive the crackling inquiry into the care and treatment
of Texas mustangs. When Bragg had concluded it he wheeled
on Boykin, ordering him uncivilly to return to his regiment
and ready it for departure within the hour. To Buck he
said, "You, sir, will stay with me."

Boykin felt obliged to spell out the superior merits of
his original plan envisioning the assignment of Miller Nalls
and Eubie Buell to work with Buck. Bragg gave him a
chilling stare.

"Have you, sir," he asked, "any sane doubts as to who is in command here? If so, or, indeed, if you wish to present any further tactical suggestions, please speak freely. I am known for my charitable attitude and open mind toward such advice from my subordinates."

Boykin smiled, spread his hands graciously. It was the sort of an eloquently delicate "no thank you, sir," which only a gentleman officer would dare offer in declining such an intimate—and deadly—invitation. In Boykin's case Bragg accepted it, source considered, and the opportunity to withdraw once more presented itself. But alert Eubie Buell saw the breach and plunged successfully into it.

"Hold on a minute, General," he requested, stepping from ranks. "If I might add a word to what the Colonel ain't said, I'd be right beholden."

Buck thought Bragg was going to have a stroke. But after a moment he got his color back and said to Eubie, in no way nasty or curt, "By all means; pray continue."

"Yes, sir, thank you, sir. Well, General, seeing as how me and the other boys here has marched with old Buck the whole way from Paint Rock Crossing of Concho River, it does seem a dirty shame to separate us on the edge of our first fight. Now if you was to reconsider, General, and leave us go on together like you ought, you would find us the ringiest one bunch of Yankee-killers you got. By God, there just ain't no other troop in the entire damned Confederate States Army no loyaler nor hotter to serve than the Concho County Comanches. You can tie that hard and fast to your saddle horn, General. She won't slip on you. We come here to fight!"

Bragg said quietly to Boykin, "Put that man in arrest."

Unpausing, he directed his sergeant orderly to run up a squad and relieve the Texans of the horses, adding bluntly for Buck to go at once to the staff picket line and bring up his mount. With that, he spun about and was gone back into his tent in the same angry way he had popped out of it. When the flaps had settled behind him Boykin looked at Buck and raised his shoulders helplessly.

"I'm sorry, son," he said. He lowered his voice. "You be careful now, you hear? Watch out for him. Don't give him any chances at you. Not any."

Before Buck could make anything of the warning, the friendly colonel of the Light Blues had faced rightabout and was addressing the Comanches.

"All right, lads, come along and don't despair. We've a whole war remaining in which to find our proper place of

service. Nothing's done which can't be undone. Lively
now . . . !"

With the cheering admonition, he marched off down the
rise. The Texas boys followed unquestioningly after him.
None of them thought to say anything of especial farewell
to Buck Burnet, and only Miller Nalls was puzzled enough
to hang back and wave hesitantly, before trotting off to
catch up with the others. As for Buck, he made nothing
greater of the affair than had his friends, imagining, as did
they, that the parting was temporary, and assuming, as had
Colonel Boykin, that an entire war lay yet ahead of them
in A. S. Johnston's Army of the Mississippi, during which
they might successfully work out for themselves a unit assignment as mounted scouts and couriers.

23   A. S. Johnston,
En Avant

WHEN BUCK RETURNED with Bragg's bay, Bragg was waiting
impatiently. Mounting up, he growled, "Stand to my stirrup
and look smart!" Buck, guessing he was supposed to go
along, ran to catch up. Five minutes later he stood on a rise
beyond the command tent, the bay in hand, all eyes for the
glittering assemblage below. A friendly Tennessee soldier
occupied the rise with him.

"Where you from?" he asked. "Not from around here,
I'll allow."

"Nope," said Buck, "Lipan Springs, Texas. That's out in
Concho County."

"Say! That's Injun country, ain't it?"

"Yup, I reckon so. Leastways I don't know any Injuns
that comes any wilder."

"Damn, that's something!" said the stocky youngster. "My
name's Sam Watkins. I'm in the 1st Tennessee and I'm
right glad to know you."

Buck nodded that the same went for him and that he was
on Bragg's personal staff.

"That's a shame," grinned Watkins, "but misery admires
company and the 1st Tennessee is one of Bragg's regiments,
too. That makes us comrades in arms, I'd say. So anything
you want to know about this here army, you ask me. I
can see you're new, and I been in since May of Sixty-one."

"I been in since April of Sixty-two," Buck smiled wryly. "You might start off by naming me some of them officers yonder. Onliest one I know is General Johnston."

"Well, he's the best," said Watkins. "He's the most beloved general in the army, I'll vow, not even excepting Robert E. Lee. Look at him stand there handsome and straight as a squirrel rifle! You ever see a general to beat him?"

Buck, studying the tall, silver-haired commander, resplendent in his long coat of Confederate gray, cavalry sash, sword belt, mid-thigh boots and gleaming golden spurs, could only shake his head.

"Not ever . . . !" he said, face alight. Then, sobered by such splendor, "How about the others?"

"Well," said Watkins, "yonder is John Hunt Morgan, the young feller with the black plume in his hat. Then there's the homely, squint-faced one in the dirty uniform. That's old Nathan Bedford Forrest. Past him there's Breckinridge and Hardee. The big fat feller with them is Colonel Matt Martin of the 23rd Tennessee. Then you got General Gladden and General Chalmers next to him, and that little feller with the dark skin and dandy outfit is one you'd ought to know, even if you're new. See him, the real black-haired, snooty-looking one with all the braid? Standing right next to Johnston there."

Buck peered hard, brightened suddenly. "By Jings," he said, "that must be General Beauregard!"

Watkins nodded acridly. "I'm afraid so," he said, "and that big feller with the gaunted-up face and wild eyes standing with him is old Bishop Polk. So there, with Bragg, is just about your high command of the Army of the Mississippi." He sighed and shook his head. "Leave me tell you it don't compare to the Army of Northern Virginia. We all cussed the day the 1st Tennessee got transferred West. Anything else you want to know, Buck Burnet?"

"Sure, but this ain't the time: meeting's breaking up yonder."

"So it is," nodded Sam Watkins. "I allow we had best get on down there."

The two boys exchanged waves, took their horses down the rise on the trot. Buck came to a stand a proper distance behind Bragg where he was taking his leave from Johnston. "Yes, General Bragg," he heard Johnston say, "that is the shape of it. I am sure you will come to agree. Now then, gentlemen, if there are no more questions . . ." He removed from his breast pocket a field map of Tennessee. Placing it upon the table before him, he wrote upon its margin in a slender, precise script: *A. S. Johnston, 3rd April 1862, ,en avant.* Then, refolding the map, he looked at his watch. "Gentlemen," he said, "it is twelve noon. Let us go forward."

"Amen," rumbled Bishop Polk. "May God attend the right."

The advance went badly from the first. The sunny mist which had warmed the Corinth staff meeting grew into a persistent light rain. The roads, already rutted from the previous storm, would not turn water. In the late afternoon, when the fall increased, Johnston's intended swift march bogged down to an inchworm crawl.

Bragg took immediate alarm. The commander of the Florida Corps suffered none of the delusions which cursed the Confederate General Staff. When the water began to back over the road and lie in sheets to the horses' hocks and midway of the foot soldiers' shanks, and when the supply wagons foundered to their hubs in the gumbo clay, the general bellowed for his horse to be brought forward. With Buck splashing at his stirrup, he rode anxiously forward to plead with Albert Sidney Johnston the imperative need for forcing on through the night to keep the advance on its agreed schedule for a Saturday dawn attack.

Johnston refused to become perturbed. "What difference, General," he inquired in his soft-voiced way, "will a day create in our tactical situation? Is it not conceded that Grant is aware of our movement?"

"Nothing is conceded!" snapped Bragg. "A day saved could mean the victory. In such weather we cannot assume Grant is aware either of our nearness or of our number. Further, there is our own information that Buell is moving down from Savannah with seventeen thousand Union men. We dare not risk delay. We must go on tonight, we cannot stop. The decision, General, waits on you. Be advised to make it with full regard to the potential of Buell."

Johnston smiled calmingly. "Come, now, General," he said, "we do not actually know where Buell is. Neither are we certain of his intentions. And, indeed, if he does mean to join Grant, our information does not indicate that he will be able to do so before we find and destroy the latter."

"Precisely! Precisely!" shouted Bragg. "If we knew where Buell was and what he intended doing, we would not be standing here in this slop haranguing the matter. It is the very fact that we do *not* have trustful information as to his whereabouts, which makes our position so critical. We simply cannot take the chance that Buell may be within the same day of our own ability to establish contact with Grant at Pittsburg Landing."

Johnston hesitated, sent forthwith for General P. G. T. Beauregard. Bragg growled like an angry dog at this move and, when he saw the Louisiana dandy mincing up through the rain, slunk off to stand sullenly apart. Buck did not fall back with Bragg but stood at attention while Johnston put the problem of Bragg's fears to the hero of Fort Sumter. To Buck's astonishment, Beauregard categorically denied both Bragg's military doubts and his grave deductions therefrom. There was absolutely no risk, said he, in resting the troops for the night. Moreover, it was absurd to suppose that Buell could get across the river and into line with Grant before they could engage and break the latter at the Landing. Therefore, to argue Buell's whereabouts became academic, and to council a forced night march, ridiculous.

Bragg was furious. He groaned as though in physical pain. Then, with a shuddering effort at control, he bowed to his two superiors, turned and said almost gently to Buck, "Come along, boy, there's no one here to listen."

Bragg did not look back but Buck saw that Beauregard and Johnston had heard the remark. They were both shaking their heads in seeming sympathetic resignation to Bragg's obstinacy. Yet the Texas boy had a feeling that Bragg was right, and that it mattered very much indeed where General Don Carlos Buell might be with his seventeen thousand fresh and well-trained troops.

24 Indecisions, 3 April

BUCK SHIVERED and tried to shrink farther back under the canvas wagon cover he had stretched between two dogwood saplings at the head of the picket line in hope of contriving dry shelter. There was no such thing to be had in the Confederate camp. Not even the generals were dry. No fires burned. No food was cooked.

Buck shook again to the chill of the night. Since his thoughts persisted in turning upon his fellow Comanches it was not strange that his heart leaped up when he heard a voice calling out incautiously, "Hey, Buck, where the hell you at?" And then a second voice, counseling fearfully, "Jesus, Eubie, hush up! You'll have us took and shot. You're supposed to be under arrest!" And Eubie's voice again, undaunted. "Well, hell, I believe I would rather be took and shot than to go on down this here line of Bragg's nags, feeling my way, blind. Hey, Buck! Sing out, damn you, we're being swept downstream!"

"Here!" cried Buck. "Just keep coming four more horses' behinds and stop when you get to an old bay bonepile which puts his hind foot through your face for your trouble. That's me squatting under the wagon tarp three bounces and a splash from where you'll land."

A moment later the two voyagers were crawling under the shelter, bear-hugging and pummeling Buck in pure delight. But the greeting wore away quickly. "Buck," said Miller Nalls, "what we going to do now? Willy Bill and Todo and Little Bit said to tell you that if you say the word, we will all of us up and run off. To hell with old Bragg. We can still make it to Richmond. What you say?"

"Miller," said Buck, "you can't run off from an army. That's desertion. We'd be shot."

Eubie shook his head stubbornly. "We didn't aim to do no foot-fighting in these parts. We joined up to go to Richmond as cavalry."

"Buck," repeated Miller Nalls, "what we going to do?"

There was silence then, for that was the real question. "I honest to God don't know," said Buck, after a long frown. "Maybe you can tell me. I been doing a lot of thinking, and it don't come out happy I can tell you."

"Thinking," said Eubie, "can make a man sick."

Again Miller asked, "What we going to do, Buck?"

Buck turned on him.

"Damn it!" he snapped. "I ain't your leader no more. Can't you get that through your thick head?"

"Buck"—Miller put his hand slowly to his friend's shoulder—"you got to help us. There ain't nobody else what can."

"Miller's right," said Eubie uneasily. "We all look to you, Buck."

"Jesus," groaned Buck, and let the slash and drive of the rain take over. Presently he said, "How's Willy Bill and the others?"

"They're fine." It was Eubie answering. "Little Bit's caught a heavy cold and is fevered some."

"Small wonder. This here rain. It's a raw one."

"Yep." The other boy exhaled. "You can see your breath. That's somewhat for April."

The talk, having got as small as it could, disappeared altogether. The boys sat looking out into the rain. It was Miller, eventually, who had a thought.

"Buck," he asked, "you feared?"

"Of what?"

"Getting kilt."

"I dunno. You?"

Miller nodded and held his head down. "Powerful," he said.

"Me, I'm feared I won't get kilt," said Eubie. "I would rather get shot than drownt any old day. And if this damn cloudburst don't let up we won't none of us need to worry about no Yanks winging us. Nor us them. You ever try getting gunpowder to go off under water, boys? Let me tell you, there's a trick to it."

"Eubie," asked Buck, "don't nothing ever faze you?"

"Oh, you're damned right it does, Buck. Now don't press me, I'll think of what it is directly."

Buck gave up. Eubie would go down grinning wherever he was when his bullet came along. Miller would be frowning, sober-faced, trying to figure things out in his clumsy way, right up to the last breath. But he would not be afraid either. Neither would Willy Bill Bearden, who by his own admission had the grit of a bear-dog. Or Little Bit Luckett, who would bet the devil hell wasn't hot. Or big Todo Mac-Lean, who would wrestle a boar grizzly barehanded. No, his boys would make it through all right. The question was Buck Burnet.

"Miller," Buck finally said, "I'm going to tell you what I think is going to happen, and I will leave it to you and the others what to do about it. As far as me being the leader, that's finished. We're a thousand miles from where we shook on that deal. We wasn't nothing but kids a thousand miles ago. Seven fellows that thought they was growed up enough to go and fight. Well, we ain't. A man being six foot tall and tough in his muscles don't make him a man in his mind and spirit. It don't grow him up inside."

He looked away from his two friends.

"Boys," he said, "there's more going on here than we got any notion of. I don't begin to understand the half of it, but one thing sure; it ain't the idea of dying that sweats me. It's the *why* of that dying that I can't think through. My mind is beginning to weary me, and my spirit to feel things I never imagined could be—doubts and fears of my inside self—and doubts and fears of what I'm doing here— that's what's got me scared."

Buck wiped his face, blue eyes shadowing over.

"I keep seeing them quality folks of Mendota dancing and carrying on at the Amon plantation. I keep hearing what that fine Alabama girl said about the war and about how only half the people are really fighting it. I can't get her off my mind, nor Cart, nor J.C. But even with them, you know what I keep seeing most? It's that poor lonesome-eyed colored man we give over to the High Sheriff at Munroe."

Eubie frowned. "Why him, Buck?" he said. "We done the best we could for him."

Buck's face twisted. He tried to marshal his answer into good hard order, but could not do it. Finally he had to begin with another headshake.

"Eubie," he said, "Miller and me ain't never told you and the other boys the truth of what happened to that colored man. I was worried you wouldn't understand it. But you know a funny thing? It was me that didn't understand it, and that didn't want to think about it, nor face square up to it."

"Buck, you're talking queer."

"No, wait. You remember when our train pulled out of Munroe?"

"Sure. Why?"

"Well, no more than half a mile out, there was a little wood trestle going over a creek. Miller and me could just see it from our seat. You other boys was on the wrong side of the car. It was him ahanging there under that trestle, Eubie, that poor scairt-sick darky. Hanging there like a strung shoat, warm-dead, with his feet adragging in the creek scum and his lonesome face turnt up like he was still singing 'Rock of Ages.'"

The stillness fell harder than the rain. After a long while Eubie said, "Well, Buck, he was took for running off three times straight."

Buck answered softly. "No, Eubie," he said, "he was took for wanting to be free. The selfsame thing you and me and Miller and all the others come a thousand miles to fight for. That's what's got me cast down and what I can't figure out."

He waited through the third stillness; then, when neither of his companions could help him, nodded wearily and took up the second half of his spirit's burden.

"Today I was with General Bragg when he rode up and told Johnston and Beauregard we was going to get whipped if we held up here. You know what Johnston did? He turned to Beauregard, asked what he thought, and Beauregard said General Bragg was daft, and Bragg turns to me and says, 'Come along, boy, there's no one here to listen,' and we got the hell out of there."

Buck lowered his voice.

"You know something, boys? They was talking about us. That's what they was *really* talking about. Us soldiers. The ones Bragg meant when he said 'we' mightn't be so lucky. He was talking about Buck Burnet and Miller Nalls and Eubie Buell. I got that belly-sink feeling. Like when it's going to blow up a blue norther, or a trail herd is going to spook and run."

Miller Nalls shivered and said, "How come you to know, Buck?"

"Because General Bragg done told me. It was back at his tent. He had forgot I was still there. Finally he looked around and seen me standing there with Old Brown and he said to me real softlike, 'Oh, I'm sorry, boy. Dismissed.'

"I saluted him proper and he called out for me to wait up a minute. Then come astomping up to me in that hunch-shouldered way he has. At last he said, friendly and kind as you please, 'Boy, you know any good prayers?'

"By Jings, I just stood there a minute, stumped. Then I up and said, yes, sir, I guessed I did, and he bobbed his beard at me, scowled black as thunder, leaned in close, thumped me hard on the chest and said, '*Say 'em then, boy, say 'em!*' And with that he slewed around and marched off stalky and mean as ever."

"Damn," said Eubie after a bit. "That's dismal."

"It scared me," said Buck.

25 The Stillness Saturday Night

THE FOLLOWING MORNING, April 4, there was no cessation of the rain. The air failed to warm as morning drew on. The troops were late getting back upon the road and by nightfall still were not up to the Union lines at Shiloh. By this time the two roads to the front were impassable to multiteam wagons and heavy guns. During the night the downpour lessened and Saturday was clearing with patchy clouds and intermittent rain scud driving across the drowned land under gusty winds.

Through the day there was some surface drainage of the roads and by late afternoon the majority of the wagons had been got up to the lines and the mired artillery pieces, under double teaming and hand-spiking, were being once more brought forward. Substantially, Johnston had his army on the ground by 4:00 P.M. By 5:00 the last division was in place. By 6:00 the lowering overcast, having shielded the Confederate final move, began to lift.

Sunset proved a glorious retreat of red, gold and purple cloud. Twilight was entirely clear. With full dark a tropic breeze came on to blow sweet and springy from the Gulf. The night turned off decidedly warm and the southern spirit rose.

Up at command headquarters, just outside the light from the wagon lamp above Johnston's map table, waited Buck Burnet with Bragg's horse. Johnston was markedly sanguine. Beauregard was more cautious but supported the optimistic view in the main. Of the others only Bragg spoke up. Was there any change, Bragg wanted to know, in the situation at present? Beauregard answered him when Johnston seemed to hesitate. The situation, he explained icily, was virtually the same, except that the attacking Confederate force was now to be one of lines of corps rather than the previously conceived formation of columns of corps. The idea was Beauregard's.

Bragg was instantly upon his feet. "What is this?" he cried to Johnston. "Lines of corps? In an army of forty thousand attacking over brush-choked terrain with a contour variation of but one hundred feet? The idea, sir, is an idiocy!"

"Are you, sir," Beauregard flared, "calling into question my mental competence, or my professional judgment? I demand an explicit answer, sir!"

"And you shall have it," replied Bragg. "I am doing both. I have no time for the amenities, General Beauregard. We have an unparalleled opportunity here. If you cannot see it, kindly do not stand in the view of those who can."

"Gentlemen, gentlemen . . ." Johnston raised his hand, nodding to Bragg. "I have conditionally approved General Beauregard's revision of my plan, General Bragg. I believe it to have considerable merit and no great danger."

"Why should it have any danger?" said Bragg bluntly.

Beauregard stepped forward. "General Johnston," he said,

"I shall no longer submit to this insulting inquisition. There is a chain of command here, I believe, and I shall see it respected, sir, or withdraw myself from it."

"Bah!" shouted Bragg, raising a bony fist in defiance. "There's no need for that, General. You shall have your respect, sir. But let me advise you to enjoy it while you may. I do not think you will relish its flavor nearly so well this time tomorrow night."

"You, sir," said Beauregard stiffly, "are a surly dog."

"Aye," growled Bragg. "But a good one."

Buck stirred restlessly. He forced his eyes shut and tried to sleep. Damn. What was keeping him awake? Had he done something he shouldn't have? Or forgotten to do something he should? He pressed his lips, frowned, thought hard.

Upon returning from the staff meeting Bragg had told him to have his horse up at 4:30, and to bring another for himself. Well, he had Old Brown and the Texas pony he had chosen for his own mount unhooked from the picket line and tethered alongside his wagon sheet. Both animals were bridled and brushed, their blankets and saddles laid to hand. So it couldn't be that. It could be the worry brought on by seeing General Bragg get ignored again at the staff meeting. Or just the plain old lonesomes for Miller and the boys. Well, a soldier had to sleep, if he was going to be worth his salt in tomorrow's fight.

Within a mile or two, each way, stretching from Polk's brigade on the left to Breckinridge's on the right, forty thousand Confederate soldiers lay worrying. Across from them, over there in the shadows of Shiloh churchyard, thirty-five thousand Federals were doing the identical thing. And the creepy part of it, the part which kept a person from closing his eyes, was the great noise of stillness arising from all those waiting men. There were three-quarters of a hundred thousand soldiers crouched inside a four-mile circle of Bragg's patched tent. Yet the only sounds Buck could hear were those of Old Brown tossing his nosebag, with here and there down the picket line a muffled stomp, a low grunting whicker, or a jingle of halter-ring.

Buck shook to the chill of the silence. Maybe it was so graveyard quiet because, like him, all the rest of those soldiers felt left alone in the last hours before the big fight. Maybe that was just a natural result of being afraid you were going to die. Maybe a fellow got to thinking of that and pulled in on himself and huddled up in his own little piece of darkness not wanting to talk to anybody. Or maybe it was that he *was* wanting to talk, *and to everybody*. Well, the hell with it. He was letting his thoughts run on. Any man could spook himself if he worked at it hard enough.

Buck sat up. He dug out his watch, scratched a match to see the time. It was only nine o'clock.

"Put out that light, soldier . . . !"

The low-voiced order leaped at him from the darkness. He dropped the match and a lank shadow slid in under the wagon sheet with him and muttered, "It's all right, it's me, kid—Mercer Barnes."

"Sarge!" whispered Buck. "By damn, I am glad to see you. Lord, Lord, I never listened to such a big quiet in my whole life. You alone?"

"Nope, I brung a friend."

"Well, I declare. Who?"

"Tellis Yeager. He's going to stand your guard till you get back."

"Back? Back from where? You're talking crazy, Sarge. This is *Bragg's* picket. You couldn't drive me off my post with a pack of bull mastiffs."

"It's the little feller, Red. Luckett, ain't that his name? He's sick and wants to see you. The company surgeon seen him just now and said he wouldn't last the night out. It's pneumonia. Double and deep. I seen it kill a man in twenty-four hours."

Buck slid out from under the wagon sheet. Barnes followed him. Tellis Yeager burrowed under the sheet, put his head back out.

"What's the password?" he whispered.

"I dunno," said Buck. "I'm only assigned to the General's horse. You'd have to ask Sergeant Rambeau up at the head of the picket."

Mercer Barnes said, "Come on, Red, and watch it. A camp gets jumpy this close to the enemy. You can get drilled by your own pickets easiest thing in the world. Step soft and close behind me."

They started off, Buck moving through the darkness with Indian stealth. At the first halt to listen for pickets, Barnes said, "You part Comanche, Red?" Buck shook his head. "No," he said, "but I learnt a thing or three from them." Barnes nodded. "You learnt 'em good," he said. "You don't make no more noise than a winnow of wind in fresh wolf fur." Buck returned the nod. "I don't aim to," he said. "Let's go."

At that time in the Southern army the men broke into small messes of their own selection, usually about five or six men to a cookfire and sleeping spot. The five Texas boys, Buck saw, had stayed together. It made him feel good and brought up a hopeful stir of the old dream that the Concho County Comanches might stick together.

"All right, Red, here we are," Mercer Barnes drawled. "I'll stand watch while you go in. Don't stretch your luck. If I whistle, you duck out the back."

Buck bent down, crawled under the gun cover. At first he could see nothing, only hear Little Bit breathing. The sound of it put a chill up his back. He clenched his teeth and said, "Hello, it's me, Buck." A familiar broad form loomed before him and big Todo said, "Jesus, Buck, glad to see you. The little feller's out of his head."

Buck found a candle and made a light, shielding it with his bent body. "Little Bit," he said to the flushed boy, "I will lay you five-to-one you don't get well."

Watching the suffused face, he thought he saw the flicker of appreciation pass over it. Then next moment he knew he had, for Little Bit reached out for his hand and said, "Five-to-one, Buck? You're a piker. I'll give you ten."

Buck took the reaching hand in his, wincing at its hot scaliness. It was like a chicken's claw, not human fingers, clutching at him and he had to force back the impulse to drop it. "Little Bit," he lied, "you're going to be all right. I've talked with the surgeon and he says you'll make it fine. I just come over to see if they was treating you decent."

"I know why you come over, Buck. And thank you for it, too, you hear?"

"Sure, I hear. Say, you know what I'm doing? Taking care of one old broke-down horse. That bay plug the General rides. All I got to do is see he's kept saddled and brought up to the tent on time. Ain't that a laugh? Me, Buck Burnet? I tell you we're all doing pretty good. You playing sick so's you don't have to shoot no Yanks tomorrow. Eubie blowing off in front of General Bragg so's he'd get arrested and kept to the rear. Me holding the old man's horse. The others thinking up God knows what to get them let off too. Why, man, we got the war half won and don't know it!"

"Buck." Little Bit's head moved slightly. "Slack off. You ain't fooling nobody." He choked, panting, fighting for breath. When the spasm had passed, he whispered, "I'm just mortal glad you come, Buck. You don't need to say a thing. Just stay a spell by my side. Could you do that, Buck? It wouldn't be long."

"Don't you fret," said Buck, "I'll bide with you long as you want. You just rest now. I'll blow out the candle."

"No!" said Little Bit sharply. "Please don't do that, Buck.
The dark is powerful frightening." He had to fight for the
breath of life again. It was several minutes, this time, before
the deep râle in his lungs slowed.

Buck leaned over, suddenly frightened. "Little Bit? You
hear me? You all right?" The sick boy tried to rally, tried
to say something. The effort brought on a third fit of suf-
focation. When it had passed and his breathing once more
resumed, Buck noticed it was very high and racy in his throat.
He tipped the candle to make sure he wasn't imagining things.
He was not. Little Bit's eyes were wide open but they had
a strange, glassy light in them. There was a froth of blood
lacing his mouth corners. His lips moved but made no sound.
Buck felt a fear grow in him which was the coldest thing he
had ever felt. He could not bring himself to touch Little Bit
after that. He could not move to clean off his face, raise
his head, or help him in any way. He was afraid of him,
deathly afraid.

"Easy now, easy," was all he could think to say.

"Buck!" The whisper was so thin it barely escaped the
stilling lips, yet it was high and sharp with a nameless
fear. "The candle has gone out . . . !"

Buck looked at the candle. Its flame burned steadily.
When he looked back at Little Bit, the ticking in his friend's
throat had stopped.

He put the candle down and drew the scant rag of soiled
blanket over Little Bit's face. He picked the candle up
again, blew it out, set it back down.

"You are right, Tobin Earl," he said, "the candle has
gone out."

Then he sat down alongside his friend on the dirt floor
of the Comanches' gun-cover tent and began to cry very
softly in the darkness.

26 The Letter Home

IT WAS BUT A SHORT WAY from Colonel Boykin's campsite
to that of Braxton Bragg. Yet to Buck it seemed five miles.
He wondered a dozen times if he had missed, in the pit-
blackness of Shiloh Wood, the thin line of staff mounts and

the single disreputable tent which composed the Spartan bivouac of the Florida Corps' commander.

It was part of Bragg's wolflike aloofness that he kept and slept alone. Except for his orderly, Wirt Rambeau; his aide-de-camp, whose name Buck knew but could never remember; and a housekeeping squad of eight stablehand troopers; he maintained not a sign or symbol of corps command about him. He covered himself only with the patched and miserable Union dog-tent which was his familiar and widely feared field headquarters.

It was upon this ominous landfall that Buck Burnet finally stumbled. He still had a wagon-sheet shelter to reach, an unwilling Georgia corporal to relieve.

Sergeant Wirt Rambeau sometimes did and sometimes did not conduct the 10:00 P.M. inspection of the General's picket line. But Buck was no more than back under his wagon sheet and Corporal Tellis Yeager departed safely from it, than Rambeau came feeling his way down the picket line.

"Who goes there?" challenged Buck, in his nervousness jumping it out far too loudly.

Rambeau said brusquely, "Shut up, you damn fool. What you trying to do, wake up Crazy Sherman?"

"Crazy who?" Buck asked.

"Sherman. Grant's favorite general. Our scouts just come in and said we got Sherman right acrost the crick."

"Ain't he one of their real big fighters?"

"Middling, I reckon. He's Grant's pet. That gives him the edge. Sort of like Beauregard with Johnston."

"If he's so good, how come them to call him crazy?"

"Dunno exactly. Bragg says he ain't. Says Sherman's crazy like a hydrophoby skunk. Bragg don't like him. Says it's hard to fight a man who will run like a yellow dog one minute and turn on you like a wild bull the next."

"Um," said Buck.

Rambeau sat down on a rock. "Say, kid," he continued, "we got a dispatch rider going to Corinth in an hour. You want to send out a letter or mail some other little 'membrance home, I'll see it gets in the pouch. Remember, have it writ or wrapped before eleven o'clock. Craney will come by and pick it up about then."

Buck understood that this was gracious and kind, even risky, and told the older man as much. Rambeau refused the appreciation gruffly. "Well, thank you very much, no matter," said Buck politely. "I'm beholden for the thought."

"Damn the thought," said Rambeau. "I got a kid my own going on sixteen. How old are you, boy?"

"Seventeen."

"I thought so. You get that letter writ." Rambeau looked at him, shook his head, got up to leave.

"Sergeant," Buck said hurriedly, "you didn't say if the scouts brung in any other information from acrost the crick. Say like might help a man if he got lost, or cut off, or maybe hurt out there tomorrow. You know . . ."

He made a vague, self-conscious gesture off toward the Federal lines and Rambeau scowled and said, "Yeah, kid, I know. It's a poor country to fight in, I'd say. Low. Marshy. Flat. Lots of underbrush, shag timber, swamp grass. It will be mostly tree-to-tree small arms fire with the artillery dropped anywhere they want to drop it. We'll get hit by our own big stuff as much as by the Yanks', and them the same."

He tapped the dottle of his pipe into the palm of his hand. "Advice?" he said. "Well, yes. You get caught in a hot fire, rifle or cannon, you hunt yourself a hole and you hang in it. If it's already holding a Yank he will move over for you, never fear. You got no idea how friendly things can get when there ain't no officers around. Remember that idea of digging in, and whatever you do, kid, don't try to be a hero. It's like Mercer Barnes says, it pays the poorest of any work there is."

"Yes, sir," said Buck, "I remember him saying that. Thank you very much for reminding me."

Again Rambeau was gruff with him.

"The hell," he said. "Get busy. You will find pencil and paper in the General's right-hand saddlebag pocket. You got a candle?" Buck said he did. "Use it careful, then," ordered Bragg's sergeant. "You know the penalty for a light on the line." Again Buck acknowledged his understanding and Rambeau started back up the picket line toward the hooded glow of the General's bull's-eye lantern.

Buck got the pencil and paper from the General's saddlebag pocket. He arranged three sticks in a crude facsimile of an Indian lodgepole frame, and hung his coat over them. Inching head and shoulders inside the makeshift tipi, he struck match to candle and settled frowningly to the task of writing his letter home:

Dear Grandpa and Grandma,
    I am fine and hope you are the same.

> We had a dandy trip out and no trou-
> ble. There is to be a fight here tomorrow
> we are told.
>   Your loving grandson, Buck

To this he added the date in the left-hand corner and
the underlined words, "Shiloh Church, Tennessee," in the
right. Then he folded the paper three times over, put it
into one of Bragg's cheap brown envelopes, addressed it to
"Mr. and Mrs. James R. Burnet, Lipan Springs, Paint Rock
P.O., Concho County, Texas," and sat back to wait for
Corporal Craney and the Corinth mail.

When Craney came up minutes later Buck was sound
asleep, the letter dangling from one hand over a drawn-up
knee, the forgotten candle still sputtering under the stick-
and-coat tipi. Craney shook his head and stooped to ease
the letter free of Buck's grasp. Feeling under the coat he
pinched out the candle, then picked up the coat and laid
it carefully about Buck's shoulders. Stepping back he looked
down at the sleeping seventeen-year-old another moment.

"Jesus," he said softly, and turned away.

27   Sunday, 6 April, 1862

OLD BROWN THREW up his head and sampled the freshening
dawn wind. Then he stomped a splayed forefoot and whicker-
ed. Buck Burnet sat up rubbing his eyes. Old Brown snorted
loudly and the Texas pony tied next to him shied away wild
as a buck deer. Buck fumbled for his watch, cupped a match
against the breeze. It was 4:15 A.M.

At 4:25 he was in front of Bragg's tent with Old Brown
and the Texas pony. Bragg came out blinking and grumbling
at 4:35. There were a half dozen regimental colonels and two
brigadiers waiting to see him. He pushed them aside and took
his horse from Buck. Mounting up, he said, "By the right
flank, boy. Look sharp," and set off at a jarring trot across the
rise to Johnston's camp. His distraught adjutant ran a few
steps after him asking instruction for the waiting officers.
Bragg waved back petulantly. "Tell the fools to go forward!"
he shouted.

At Johnston's tent the general staff was assembled, though not yet mounted. Beauregard and Bishop Polk flanked the commander as usual. Bragg nodded to Johnston and requested him to step aside with him a moment.

Out of earshot of the others he jabbed a thumb in Buck's direction and said, "Now if you want me, General, yonder's my courier with the yellow horse. I will ask you to keep him with you, for I shall not send another to take his place."

From the slight rise upon which Johnston's camp was situated, was to be had the best view of the terrain over which the Southern advance must be made. Toward the east the darker line of bigger trees marking the Tennessee River curved away above Pittsburg Landing a mile and a half on their right. On their left, at an equal distance, ran the paralleling, lesser foliage of Owl Creek. Straight ahead two and a half miles, joining Owl Creek with the river and making a three-sided water trap, stretched the swamp-rank growth of big Snake Creek. Within that trap now waited thirty-five thousand Federal troops; four solid miles of Union soldiers braced in a drawn bow whose bent tips were Pittsburg Landing and Owl Creek, whose deeply pulled string was the marsh-grown Snake, and whose notched arrow was lonely, log-walled Shiloh Church. Four steel miles of men, cannon, caissons and canisters. And Buck Burnet, looking down upon their ominous number, could see absolutely nothing.

Braxton Bragg had better eyes. Turning, with a last stare at the mist-shrouded stillness below, he nodded abruptly to Johnston. "If we are to carry this field," he said, "it will need to be done today. I can tell you, sir, that Buell is presently outside Savannah asking to be brought across the river. My scouts brought in that information just now. Let us remember, General, that Savannah is but nine miles by the river, twelve by land on the longest road. These are fresh troops, sir. They are not marched out and the roads are drying." For a final moment he looked off over the brooding silence of Shiloh Wood. "You must not stop for *anything*, General Johnston," he said, "and I *will not* do so. Good day to you, sir."

He had saluted and turned away before Johnston could think to reply. Then, however, the latter called out after him in a voice of patent cheer and one, as well, sufficiently strong to carry its message of confidence to his listening staff, "General Bragg, sir, do not worry I beg of you. To-night we will water our horses in the Tennessee River!"

Buck waited with his little Texas pony, lost in the swirl of staff personnel eddying about Albert Sidney Johnston. He had no idea of his course of duty except to follow the Confederate command wherever the advance might lead it, keeping himself ready to ride for Bragg's lines upon the instant. He wandered, presently, over to the rocky point where Bragg had stood with Johnston, staring at the Union stillness. Suddenly he stiffened, every nerve in him going tight. The dawn had grown, the mists retreating from the low creeks and water oak ponds below. Now he could see.

Those were Confederate men down there! And not moving by twos, or threes, or squads of eight, or even skirmish lines of company strength. From Owl Creek to the river, the undergrowth of Shiloh Wood was alive with Rebel infantry. Buck was looking at thousands—tens of thousands—of Southern soldiers swarming noiselessly in upon the Union lines. As he crouched, paralyzed with the enormity of the sight, a Rebel yell echoed from the extreme right upon the river. Buck wheeled and bolted for his pony.

He was in time to join the spurring mounted dash, led by Johnston on his famous horse, Fire-eater, back to the lookout point. At the very edge of the decline the commander slid his mount to a rearing halt. As he did so the Confederate artillery opened.

The first eight-pound solid shot went screaming immediately over their position and a cheer went up from the assembled Southern officers which lifted the short hairs of Buck's neck. Johnston only smiled. Not even looking around at the aroused members of his staff, he ordered quietly, "Note the hour, please, gentlemen."

"Yes, sir," responded his adjutant, and took up the campaign journal of Albert Sidney Johnston. The page to which he opened was already headed *Sunday, 6 April, 1862.* The time which he wrote down beneath the date was 5:14 A.M.

28   The Hornet's Nest

THE CONFEDERATE ASSAULT, first regiments, then brigades, hurled itself recklessly against the Union center. The sunken dirt road which fronted the position was being called "Blood Gully" by 10:00 A.M. By eleven the position itself had been given a name, "The Hornet's Nest," from the furious, stinging fire put up by its inspired defenders. At noon Union General Prentiss still held and at ten minutes after the hour Albert Sidney Johnston called up Beauregard.

"This position must be carried, General," he instructed his second. "We are losing time here we cannot afford. You know what General Bragg's scouts have told us of Buell."

"Yes, yes," admitted Beauregard, "and I am afraid the information was correct. I have just now been told that General Nelson is drawing up across the river with the first division of Buell. General Lew Wallace is also coming up from Crump's Landing. As you say, sir, we must indeed go forward, but I do not see how. Is there something I have overlooked?"

Johnston nodded. "Or underestimated," he said.

Beauregard flushed. "What is that, sir?" he said.

"Bragg, sir," answered Johnston quietly. "Orderly, will you kindly call over General Bragg's courier. He is that tall, red-headed boy on the dun horse."

"What do you intend?" asked Beauregard, as they waited. Johnston raised his shoulders.

"Bragg is a man who will not quit. He is just presently beyond The Hornet's Nest. If I tell him to turn for the river, he will turn for the river. And he will reach it. Prentiss will be enfiladed and must quit."

Beauregard scowled. "It will extend Bragg to do it," he objected. "Prentiss may break out, or Grant, in. I would not risk it, sir."

"General Beauregard," said Johnston softly, "I can no longer agree. Bragg was right. There is unparalleled opportunity here. We must not let it pass."

"You will press on then?"

"With every power God gives me."

Buck Burnet, coming up at the moment, was given the order for Bragg orally. Copies in writing, said Johnston, would be forthcoming. Meanwhile time was beyond price. General Bragg must turn right at once and drive through to the river. Buck saluted, ran for his horse.

From the command post elevation The Hornet's Nest was plainly visible. He knew the course he must take to reach the landward flank where Bragg had broken across Blood Gully and driven beyond Prentiss on the left. His heart was high as he sent the Texas pony flying down the rise. Now he was finally to get into the fight! Now at last he would see something! And he was right. But what he saw left him stunned. Among the first of the shattered dead to block his path, sprawled in a bull-shouldered, clumsy way which clutched at his heart, lay big Todo MacLean. Buck's initial shock deepened into physical sickness.

He came, uncaring, to Blood Gully. The Union and Confederate dead lay so thickly together in the sunken roadway before him that his pony would not take the bank. Buck turned him away, following the road until a point was reached where the dead were not so many and a clear path among them might be picked with care. As he tried sealing his eyes to the dead, so he tried deafening his ears to the dying. He would not listen to their cries for medical aid, or one mouthful of water, or a merciful bullet through the brain. He would not look at, would not believe, the various agonies of hurt and dismembering mutilation which assailed him on every side. No, he did not see these things, they did not exist, they could not exist.

But they did, and Buck Burnet knew they did. His mouth twisted. Good Lord, he thought, I don't actually know what I am doing here. I have marched a thousand miles from home and three days through the mud and rain from Corinth and seen two friends dead in the past twenty-four hours and I don't know where I am or what I am doing here. Well, sure, he corrected himself, he was here to fight Yankees. But why? Over what? What had they done to him? Or to his? Nothing, absolutely nothing.

The answer compounded Buck's bewilderment. He sat motionless on the dun pony while the minutes fled and the sounds of battle died away to a rumble on his far right and a thin crackle on his distant left. As he waited, a party of Union officers rode out of the timber north of his hiding place.

The officers stopped their horses not twenty feet from the jack oak copse in which Buck sat his mustang. They gave it a glance and that was all. It was too small for anything more. The luck of the wind lay also with Buck Burnet; it was away from the Union horses, toward his Texas mount. The yellow pony stood to it without twitching an ear.

Buck watched the officers scan the wooded fields to the east with their field glasses, toward the Tennessee River and the Confederate flank of General Braxton Bragg. He heard them begin to talk shortly and with some excitement, the exchange revealing that they considered Bragg dangerously extended, and that a swift, bold strike at his rear might at this stage be decisive. One of their number, a short, rumpled man in a rankless uniform and private's forage cap, shook his blunt head in qualification of the company opinion.

"Not decisive, gentlemen," he suggested, "imperative. Prepare the order, Major," he said to the officer beside him.

The latter turned to obey but the order to strike at Bragg's rear was never drawn. A messenger at that instant dashed across the field with a halloo which penetrated Buck's befuddlement like a rifle bullet.

"General Grant, sir! General Grant! General Sherman has held at Shiloh Church, sir, but begs to report he cannot long continue to control the men without help! He does not want troops but pleads that you come personally if you are able. The men are calling for General Grant, sir, all along the lines. General Sherman says he believes it will be the difference if you are able to come."

The Union commander's face showed no expression beyond that of thoughtful concentration. He puffed on his cigar for some time, nodded to the courier and said, "Tell General Sherman the difference will be along directly." Then to his aide he added tersely, "A fresh cigar, please, Major. This one has lost its flavor."

The Union staff moved off following the same course which had brought it into the clearing. As the last of its members disappeared Buck drove the yellow mustang out of the jack oak copse and away in a wild gallop in the opposite direction. Minutes later he found Bragg with the information that his left flank was cleared of Union troops and Grant gone off to bolster Sherman in front of Hardee and Polk. Bragg turned at once and struck for the river. Within the hour Prentiss was enfiladed.

Yet, singularly, the surrender did not come. The gallant Union commander continued to hold back the Confederate center, giving Foote time to flank Breckinridge from the river with his gunboats. When Prentiss at last sent his aides to wait on the victorious Confederate commanders he had remaining a mere two thousand two-hundred men, and the gesture was bitter ashes in the mouth of A. S. Johnston. The Hornet's Nest had held. Grant had won the morning.

29 Tragedy at 3:00 P.M.

ONE P.M. Eight hours, now, and the attack blazed on. Bragg and Breckinridge were up to the Union siege guns at the Landing. From the river Foote's gunners on the *Tyler* and *Lexington* shredded the shore growth which shielded the gray host, cutting down the Confederate infantry like cordwood. Ashore, the crash of the Federal siege cannon at Corinth was so shattering that spoken commands could not be heard and officers communicated with their men by hand signal. Companies disappeared. Regiments were shot away. Brigades dissolved. Entire divisions were torn apart. Still the Corinth twelve-pounders and Flag Officer Foote's pestilential gunboats crossed their fire into the packed ranks of the Confederate right. Shortly, Bragg had to delay and send up to Johnston for diversionary relief. Some pressure had got to be brought at once, he said, from the landward side.

Buck had this message directly from Bragg's hand. The officer was hollow-eyed. He stared at the Texas boy as though he had never seen him before. "Here," he rasped, "get this up to General Johnston. Tell him I shall not go forward or backward on this front until ordered in writing. Tell him I am bled white but will hold on."

Buck took the dispatch and saluted. Bare minutes later he was back at the command post with Johnston and the Confederate staff. But stubborn Bragg had waited too long. His call for a demonstration on his left, brought at the proper time, could have been answered by any one of four divisions. Now the Southern assault was losing momentum all along the line. The calculated strategy had necessarily taken Confederate command attention from the Union right at the precise time that Grant had chosen to leave Prentiss and bolster Sherman from Shiloh Church to Owl Creek.

Meanwhile the prophecy of Sherman had borne iron fruit along the Federal right. Grant had arrived in the last thin pinch of time to halt the headlong desertion of Union troops draining Sherman to death on the landward flank. He rode along the weakening Northern lines in full view and small-

113

arms range of the enemy, and the effects upon the Federal morale were incalculable.

Men cheered him until their throats would utter no further sound. They died for him as though it were a privilege. Cowards who had run behind Sherman and McClernand stood like heroes before Grant.

He had his first horse killed under him with a rupturing hit from a Confederate Parrot Gun. He rode the dying animal to the ground, stepping off him and alighting with cigar ash in place and voice raised only sufficiently to carry to his aide above the roar of the dueling artillery. "Another mount, please, Major. A stouter one this time, if you will."

In an adjacent section of the line a charge of canister carried away his hat. Still further along, a fragment of shell ripped a foot-long slash under the arm of his coat, grazing his ribs. A Kentucky rifle slug slammed into the shoulder-strap which should have carried his general's rank and which some say did not even show a second lieutenant's insignia that day. Yet later a third missile hit his saddle, plowed up through the tough wood of the tree, and ended its flight unbelievably nestled in his coat pocket. He was talking to the 41st Illinois at the time, calming them into a return to the line. Hundreds of blue troopers saw and heard that bullet strike. When Grant then reached into his pocket and brought the spent lead into view, the response from his powder-grimed listeners was thunderous.

It went that way from one end to the other of the reviving Northern front. Grant struck the spark and the weary Union troops caught fire. The Confederate attack faltered, failed to gain, came on once more and receded. The Union held the field from Shiloh Church eastward to the end of battle.

When Buck came up to Johnston with Bragg's request for relief on the right, the Confederate commander was in the act of issuing an order recalling Bragg to bolster the left. The implication was not lost even upon a three-day recruit. The Confederate Army of the Mississippi was in trouble, flank to flank.

TWO P.M. and stalemate. The Southern assault had fallen away on all fronts. From Foote's floating anchor on the Tennessee River to W.H.L. Wallace's battered, bloody corner-stone at Owl Creek the Union line stretched unbroken. This was the critical hour for the Confederates. Johnston was consumingly aware of it.

Bragg meanwhile had come to wait upon his commander

as directed. As soon as he saw Johnston he demanded to know who was the author of the order pulling him out from the right. Johnston did not beg the question. Beauregard, he answered. Bragg replied angrily that he had thought as much; then went on to say he would obey the order under written protest. On the other hand, if he were permitted to stay where he was, he could guarantee to hold with what he had until Grant gave on the left. There the Union lines must yield to sustained Confederate pressure. In the attack to supply that pressure he would act as the river pivot for the Confederate giant swing which would drive loose the Owl Creek flank of W.H.L. Wallace. This done, the siege guns could be taken from behind and Bragg could move on the Landing. With the Landing went the day. If Beauregard's order to take Bragg out from the right were allowed to stand, General Johnston had lost the Battle of Shiloh. Let him weigh that chill fact in the balance of his warm regard for the gentleman from Louisiana.

Brutal and blunt as the reminder was, Johnston felt the icy certainty of truth which lay in it. "Gentlemen," he said, forestalling the glaring Beauregard, "let me have a moment to myself. The choice is not without peril, as we all realize."

He walked off a short distance and stood, head down, hands clasped behind his back, a sad and lonely figure in that silent moment. He proved, however, peculiarly quick with his decision. When he returned it was evident he had sought and received inspiration from a source beyond that dreary field.

"Gentlemen," he announced, "we shall go forward. General Bragg, if you will be so good as to hold on the right, we shall endeavor to turn the left for you. General Beauregard, sir, let us go. I should like to lead the center myself."

Shortly before 2:30 P.M. General Albert Sidney Johnston reached the right center of the Confederate line east of Shiloh Church. He stood in his stirrups waving to the cheering troops, clear voice ringing out the last order: *"Once more and we have them, lads!"* Then he put Fire-eater in front of the nearest gray-clad regiment and swung him out across the shell-churned earth. Behind him the roar of his men crashed like salvo upon salvo of massed artillery. The Southern front erupted. Nothing human could hold against it.

The hell of battle had resumed not quite half an hour, the aroused Confederates carrying the Federals back upon their reserves at every division point along the line, when, at ten minutes before 3:00 P.M., a ricocheting Minié ball cut across the ham of Johnston's leg. The wound was considered super-

ficial. Johnston, urged to send for his surgeon, said no, insisting
the latter was busy with more grievous injuries than his own.
He signaled to those about him to continue forward, and put
his mount once more in the van to set them the example.
Within a hundred yards he swayed in the saddle. He was
caught as he fell and taken to the shelter of a nearby ravine.
There, beneath a screening oak, he was laid upon the April
grass to rest. It was still thought he had fainted from fatigue
more than from the loss of blood occasioned by his injury.
But he had not. When the staff surgeon hurried up at three
o'clock, Albert Sidney Johnston was dead.

The Yankee missile had severed the femoral artery in his
thigh, and Pierre Gustave Toutant Beauregard was now in
command of the Confederate fate at Shiloh Church.

30   Last of the Light
Blues

BEAUREGARD at once sent an order down to Bragg: pull out
on the right, cross over in the rear, go back in on the left.
Buck Burnet carried the order and Bragg did not contest it.
Handing Buck the written acknowledgment, he said, "All
right, it is useless here anyway. Tell General Beauregard I
shall be in line by 4:30. And, boy . . ." Buck had already
turned away when Bragg barked after him, "When you have
told him you may return and seek out your friends." He
walked over to Buck, lowering his voice to be sure he was
not overheard in the kindness. "You have done well enough,
lad. Besides, I want no more messages than necessary from
General Beauregard. He will quit as soon as dark will decently
let him. You come back and go on with us, boy. That's where
the honor will be when the sun goes down tonight."

Bragg pulled out his watch. "Three-forty," he noted. "I
should be crossing behind the center about 4:10. You may
join there. It will save you a few Yankee shots."

Buck, who had had his coat holed twice, his boot ripped
at the ankle and his cheek laid open by stray Union lead,
winced and answered, "Thank you, General Bragg, sir."

Bragg deepened his scowl. "Go along, boy," he said.
"Beauregard will think I have bolted the order, or the field,
or both. Johnston's dead and this day is lost with him."

He passed a hand over his face, wearily, and Buck noticed

how pale he was. When he went on he talked as though he had forgotten Buck.

"It is," he said, "unless we can drive in the Federal right, smash Wallace loose from Owl Creek, turn him and go in behind that siege battery at the Landing. That is perfectly obvious now, of course, even to *him*. But by the time Beauregard understands something . . ." He let the thought hang, finished hoarsely, "God help us; everything has gone wrong."

Buck began edging nervously away. Bragg shot out a long arm, clutching him by the shoulder. "Did he suffer, lad?" he asked. "Did he die hard? How did it happen? Did you see it?"

"No sir," said Buck, "I didn't see it. But I was told that it was amazing. General Johnston just laid down and went. One minute he was acting normal, the next he was stretched out gray as a beached fish. The surgeon said he could have saved him easy as bandaging a cut finger had he got to him ten minutes sooner."

"A black tragedy," said Bragg. "But for Beauregard a blessing."

"Sir?" said Buck, surprised.

"I would have had the command save for that Creole devil!"

"Oh."

At this moment Wirt Rambeau came up to report some other business to Bragg, and Buck took the opportunity to start for his yellow pony. But he had no more than taken up the reins before Rambeau had finished with Bragg and was waving for Buck to wait. When he came up he began fussing with the dun's flankstrap and said, "Pretend to be working on this with me; he's watching." Buck understood and fell to the game.

"Now then," said Rambeau, "I seen Mercer Barnes a bit ago and he asked me to tell you that Colonel Boykin and all the officers of the Light Blues are either dead or down and that he's commanding what's left of the regiment, less than a hundred men. Bragg brevetted him at The Hornet's Nest. A lieutenant. Can you beat that?"

"Sarge, that ain't what Barnes told you mainly to tell me, is it?"

"No," he said, "it ain't. He told me to tell you that the gangly, freckle-faced feller with the crooked teeth was gone. Six-pound solid shot took him low; knocked off both legs at the hips. He went merciful quick."

"Oh, Jesus, no," groaned Buck. "Not Willy Bill."

"That's the one. Mercer claimed he never seen such grit

in twelve years of soldiering. Said the kid lived four, five minutes clear and conscious, knowing he was going to die the whole time. Talked normal to the end, never once whimpering or letting on he *did* know. Last thing he said was, 'Well, boys, I've lost the trail. Tell old Buck the beardog's gone home and will wait for him by the river.' "

"I can't believe it, Sarge," said Buck. "First Little Bit, then Todo, now old Willy Bill. All three in not even one day, and here's me with only a scratch on my cheek. Why, I ain't even thought about getting hurt. Sarge, it ain't right; it just ain't right."

"That ain't all neither," said Wirt Rambeau quietly. "The little smart-alec towhead, he's gone too."

Buck stared at him blankly. "No," he said, shaking his head, "not old Eubie. He's not dead."

"The same as," said Rambeau. "He's missing."

Buck never saw Eubie Buell again. He saw Miller Nalls late that afternoon as Bragg got his corps back in line on the Confederate left. Miller was with Mercer Barnes and had on a corporal's shirt. Tellis Yeager was also there, wearing Barnes' old blouse with its sergeant's chevrons. Barnes himself had taken a dead lieutenant's dove-gray shortcoat and was wearing it over his undershirt, which was hanging in powder-burned tatters. Sick as he was, and despairing, Buck could not keep back a lopsided grin, nor a wry greeting, as he stumbled up to report.

"Begging your pardon, sir," he said to Barnes, saluting him twice. "William Buckley Burnet, the only private soldier in the Confederate Army reporting for duty, sir."

"Red!" Barnes cried. "By God, kid, I *am* glad to see *you!* Damn, oh damn. We seen that yellow horse of yours laying on the ridge yonder and figured you was gone up for sure."

"Rode square into a Yank patrol this side of the bottom draw," said Buck. "That little horse ran five hundred yards up the ridge with eight, ten bullets clean through him. . . . Say!" he said in sudden indignation, "you know something? I been getting shot at all the damned day long and ain't fired a round back yet!"

"You come to the right place to remedy that," nodded Barnes. "Tellis, issue this man a gun."

Yeager stepped ten feet to the nearest dead soldier, stooped, took up his rifle, tossed it to Buck.

"Wear it in good health," he advised humorlessly.

Over across the cowpath which cut the woods to their right, seventy-eight hollow-eyed survivors of the grim reaping before The Hornet's Nest lay or crouched in the drying mud waiting for Lieutenant Mercer Barnes to get them again upon their feet and moving forward. The latter, seeing Buck's glance, gestured him aside.

"Red," he said, "we got to go and put them men on their feet or they're done. We're still supposed to be with Bragg and to stay up with him but his own aide was by here half an hour ago looking for him. He said Bragg was giving the same answer to all officers: put your men in any place and go forward; all stragglers to be shot where found."

He looked over at the exhausted troops and grimaced angrily. "Goddamit, Red," he said, "this is a real bad tangle, and I've seen a few that were Lulus. This army is scrambled worse than a box of dropped eggs. That son of a bitching Creole genyus with his 'lines of corps'! Oh, that Loozyanna Boneypart! I tell you I would love to have him back of a clump of jack oak for about five minutes. Jesus, Jesus . . ."

He trailed off hopelessly, waved for Miller and Tellis Yeager to come up. When they had he said quickly, "Let's go, boys. And stay close up to me. You three are all I got left to look out for."

Buck followed him and the others across the road, strangely affected by what Barnes had just said. It made him think once more of himself and of what had brought him up to this April day so far from home and the dream of gallant service he had seen that long-ago night in the first camp across the Concho. What had happened since then?

He glanced at Miller Nalls. The other boy was trudging along at his side saying nothing either of happiness or complaint, but Buck could read his mind as though he had a window in his head. Miller was happy. He was once more with Buck Burnet and that was all he had ever asked for as long as Buck could remember back into their Lipan Springs boyhood. Miller looked up. He smiled when he saw Buck watching him and nodded his big round head as if to say he understood and agreed with whatever Buck was thinking. With the smile he moved closer in and put his arm about Buck's shoulders, patting him comfortingly. Then in the direct, dead simple way only Miller could, he answered all Buck's doubts.

"Well, Buck," he said, "you still got me."

Bragg went in against W.H.L. Wallace at Owl Creek on the Union right at 4:30 P.M. His men fought as though there were no day to come. They stormed and breached Wallace's center, drove slashingly for his rear. The blue troops recoiled, then split, before the gray wedge, and Braxton Bragg was behind the Federal right flank.

News of the breakthrough raced the Southern lines. The Confederates began to go forward at all positions except that at the Landing. Blood Gully, Lick Creek, Church Road, Shiloh Chapel, all were put behind. At a few minutes past five o'clock W.H.L. Wallace was killed. At once his command broke. Bragg went in for the finish. With word of Wallace's death came rumor that Bragg was in sight of Snake Creek bridge and Grant had ordered his center back at last. Full of the scent of the kill, the entire Confederate Army rose up and rushed in.

Yankee boys by the hundreds were throwing down their guns to stand with raised hands where they could be seen and allowed to surrender. The Southerners streamed by them, unheeding. Buck went with the pack, running, shooting, hallooing, rebel-yelling and screaming insults with the rest. He ran until his lungs would no longer give him breath and his throat, parched shut by the acrid bite of cannon smoke and rifle stink, would not open to pass his crazed shouts. He staggered and fell over a blasted hickory giant into the pock hole of the artillery shell which had felled the big tree. The hole was waist-deep and solidly covered over with the upper foliage of the hickory. Buck remembered crashing through this roof of branches into the soft dirt at the bottom of the hole, and starting, automatically, to get up and go on. Then he was struck from behind and all light, sound and excitement of battle ceased.

When Buck awoke it was dark. The sting of cold rain was striking his upturned face. At first he did not realize where he was, then remembered falling into the shellhole beneath the downed hickory. For a time he lay unmoving, listening hard, trying to think.

Over by the river Grant's siege guns boomed on below the Landing. Out upon the stream the Federal gunboats continued their incessant shelling of the Confederate anchor above the heavy shore battery. To the north, toward Snake Creek bridge and Pittsburg Landing Road, the Union artillery still snarled defiantly. The guns sounded quite near. Startlingly so. They must, Buck thought, be set just across the road. If this were true it could mean but one thing: the Yankees had rallied from their rout and re-formed. And if *this* were true it could mean but one other thing: the battle was not over but would rage again with daylight.

The thought made Buck weak. He sat up unsteadily. At

once his head pained him severely, restoring the memory that he had been struck from behind after falling into the hole. No sooner had he recalled the fact than a familiar, cynical voice was verifying it.

"It was a shiftless, no account trick, Red, but you seemed bound to rise up and fight on and I reckoned you had ought, rather, to set a spell and think it over."

"Sarge!" cried Buck. "It wasn't you belted me?"

"It was, Red. You was bolting with the bit in your teeth. We could hear you snorting half a mile off."

" 'We'?" said Buck. "You got Tellis with you?"

"No more than you got Miller Nalls."

It was the first time Buck had thought of Miller since the charge began.

"Don't let it fret you, Red," Barnes said. "Nalls, he didn't no more think of you than you did of him. You can win bets on that all winter."

Buck knew better. Miller *had* thought of him.

He felt his stomach pull up and turn pinchy. Presently he said, "Say, Sarge, if it ain't Tellis we got in here with us, who is it?"

"Red," Barnes finally replied, "there's an old soldier's rule that when the artillery is laid flat in your face and the Minié balls are spitting past your ears hotter than splatter fat at a fish fry, there ain't no such thing as an enemy."

"What!" gasped Buck incredulously. "You meaning to tell me we got a Yank in this here hole with us?"

"I ain't *meaning* to tell you nothing, Red." Barnes' voice was flat. "I *am* telling you. We not only got a Yank in this here hole with us, but if you don't like the idea you can haul out and go find yourself a better burrow and be damned on the way."

But the fight had gone out of Buck Burnet. "Hello, Yank," he sighed. "Welcome to the old plantation. Greetings from the last of the Light Blues."

"Hello, Reb," answered a shy, friendly voice. "Same to you from the worst of the 41st."

"You get separated? Hurt, maybe, or cut off?"

"No, I got scared, Reb."

"Anybody but a natural-born hero would," put in Mercer Barnes. "That was something out there."

"It's not what I mean," said the Northern boy. "I been hiding under this tree since noon."

"Oh," said Mercer Barnes.

Presently the patter of the rain increased. More of it began to get through their roof of broken branches. Buck held out his hand and caught a few drops in his upturned palm. "You reckon," Buck said, "that it's going to rain?"

"Tastes like it," offered Mercer Barnes. "What you think, Yank?"

The Union boy was quiet a moment, then said impulsively, "I thank God I didn't shoot any of you fellows out there today."

"It ain't what I asked you," Barnes reproved the blue trooper.

"I know it's not," said the other. "But it's what I had to answer."

"All right," Barnes said, "you've answered it. Now how about the rain?"

The gentle-voiced youth turned his face up to the raindrops now virtually pouring through the leafy cover and said quietly, "Seems like a good chance, Sergeant."

"Seems like," grunted Barnes.

"Jesus," said Buck miserably. "I wish to hell we knew this country better. Might be a chicken shed or a shoat pen of some kind we could get under."

"I know the country around here," volunteered the Northern boy. "We've been camped here the best part of a week. Just up the road from this hole is the old church. We could get in there likely."

"Shiloh Church?" asked Buck, a curious feeling of past uneasiness coming up within him.

"Who cares what church?" said Barnes. "A roof's a roof. Yank, you sure you can find your way in this here cow's-belly black?"

"I'm sure, Sergeant. It's only a little ways."

The three soldiers climbed out of the shellhole. The storm lashed at them as though it had been waiting for them. They crouched back against the hickory's blasted bole, peering to get their bearings in the outer darkness. The rain sheeted down. The wind drove it at them in winnowing, spring gale gusts, striking the April cold into their bones, reducing the limit of vision to the length of an outstretched arm.

"Whew!" sputtered Buck. "This is fierce. You can't see four feet. We'd get lost from one another the first turn of the trail."

The Northern boy felt quickly through the shrouding rain. He found Buck's broad, wet shoulder.

"Give me your hand, Johnny Reb," was all he said.

31 Shiloh Church

THE CHURCH WAS DARK. It stood in an opening of the forest just off the road, a small, huddled building, the sunken flanks of its warped roof glistening eerily in the ghost light of the rain. When the lightning flashed, its afterglare fled chillingly along the bone-white phosphorescence of the churchyard pickets, lit briefly and flickered out among the weed-grown graves and lurching headstones.

"Sarge," said Buck, "I don't want to go in there. Let's turn back."

"There's no place to turn," said Barnes. "Come on."

Buck and the Yankee boy followed him past the sagging gate toward the worn hollows of the wooden doorstep. The rough plank door, wet and swollen with the rain, was closed but not latched. It yielded raspingly to Barnes' shoulder. Buck, last in, closed the door. The darkness seemed like that of the pit. They stood in it, suddenly afraid.

To Buck, the sightless dark in that country church at Shiloh, Tennessee, held and hid a menace which seized him instantly, and would not be shaken off. There was *something* in there with them. "Sarge," he whispered, "you, too, Yank; hold your breaths."

He heard their breathing stop with his own. But the sibilance of an invisible respiration continued to rise through the thickened silence.

Buck fumbled in his pocket, found the waterproof shell-case which held his remaining matches. "I'm going to make a light," he said. The scrape of the match was damp and punky, but it ignited. He raised its fitful smolder, cupped in his hands and held toward the nameless sound. The match flame steadied, flared once, died back and went out. From rear pew to front, from window aisle to window aisle, Shiloh Church was filled with crouching, fearful-eyed Confederate stragglers.

"Friend," said a soft Southern voice out of the returned darkness, "don't strike no more lights. Bragg's boys are on the road and we don't aim to draw them here."

"We ain't looking for nothing but a dry roof till daybreak,

soldier," Barnes said. "You can make a million dollars betting we won't scratch another match tonight."

"Sure, friend," said the soldier. "But we got to be careful. We're a long way behind the lines here. If you know Bragg, you know what he'd make of that."

"Desertion," said Mercer Barnes.

"Sure, and with any other general it wouldn't be no worse than ordinary soldiering. And it truly ain't, neither."

"*Ain't it?*" asked Barnes quietly.

Buck could hear the murmuring stir of uneasiness the remark sent through the Southern stragglers. No voice rose to answer Mercer Barnes' question, nor did any need to. The stillness had done that.

"Is there anybody here knows the Scriptures?" The voice came anxiously from the lighter gloom toward the altar where a small, dirty-paned window backed the pulpit. "I got a friend bad hurt and wanting to hear the Word."

Stillness built upon stillness in answer to the soldier's question. Buck understood. There were doubtless many of these Southern boys who could quote the Scriptures fairly well. But they knew, and Buck knew, that fairly well wasn't good enough for a man's last memory.

"Ain't there nobody at all?" asked the soldier.

Again the silence bore down. At Buck's side the Yankee boy stirred restlessly, stood up uncertainly.

"There's me," he said in his gentle voice.

More than one of the Southern troopers caught the alien nasal twang of his Northern speech, and the soft-speaking man who had asked Buck to strike no more matches said sharply, "Who's that? It ain't no Confederate. Boys, we got a blue-belly in here."

Mercer Barnes' voice grew hard. "You got a Yankee boy in here that came in with us," he said. "I can't vouch for the color of his belly to begin with, but it's bright red now."

"Don't get funny, Alabama," warned the soldier. "Ain't nobody here wants to laugh."

"What's funny," said Mercer Barnes, "about a fifty-caliber Confederate bullet hole in the belly?"

After a long pause the Southern trooper said, "Sorry, friend. Not a thing. Not even in a Yank's belly."

"Yank," came the voice from the front of the church, "you really know the Book?"

"Yes. My father was a minister of the Gospel."

"You reckon you could favor us by coming forward and praying for my friend?"

Another voice spoke quickly from the right-hand pews. "The wounded boy ain't the only one that would be beholden to hear the Word."

"He ain't by several," agreed a deep voice from the left-hand shadows. "I reckon we can all stand a little praying over."

"Amen to that," echoed a third fervent voice.

"You can't do it, Yank," said Buck, placing a protective arm about the Northern boy.

"The way he's hurt," said Mercer Barnes, "he's got to do it."

The boy said to Buck, "The sergeant's right, Johnny. Give me a hand up the aisle."

A dozen eager forms sprang from the darkness to his side. But Buck and Mercer Barnes carried him to the foot of the pulpit. There he murmured, "Help me to the lectern, please. That's where I was taught to read."

A nearby shadow moved forward. "There ain't no lectern in this church, Yank," it said. "You'll have to use the pulpit. It ain't no sacrilege down here. The lay brothers preach from it regular."

"All right," said the boy. He stood for a moment steadying himself, and the dying man struggled up on his pallet below and called out, "Cain't we risk a light for one minute, boys? There's a stub of candle yonder on the altar. Just for a flicker or two. I would dearly love to see his face. Only just see it . . ."

"Hold on!" rasped a hidden voice, harsh with alarm. "How about Bragg?"

Mercer Barnes said softly, "Damn Bragg," and found the candle and brought it back to Buck Burnet. Buck lit it and set it on the edge of the pulpit where its tiny blow shone upward across the features of the Yankee boy. There was an audible sound of indrawn breath.

The boy's face was pale, fair-skinned, wide-browed. His dark eyes were luminous with pain, his gaunt cheeks hollow with suffering. His hair, uncut for many weeks, fell nearly to his shoulders. It was a brown color, soft and lustrous, like his young beard. There was about his gentle mouth, parted now in glad anticipation of the chance to say a last word to these frightened men, a strange, unreal beauty.

As the silence fell again the Northern youth began to pray for the dying man, on the floor, and for all his comrades

crouching in the rainswept darkness of that long ago Sunday
night at Shiloh Church, Tennessee:

"And he opened his mouth, and taught them, saying,

"Blessed are the poor in spirit: for theirs is the kingdom of heaven.

"Blessed are they that mourn: for they shall be
comforted.

"Blessed are the meek: for they shall inherit the
earth. . . .

"Blessed are the peacemakers: for they shall be called
the children of God. . . .

"Love your enemies, bless them that curse you, do
good to them that hate you, and pray for them which
despitefully use you, and persecute you;

"That ye may be the children of your Father which
is in heaven: for he maketh his sun to rise on the evil
and on the good, and sendeth rain on the just and on
the unjust. . . ."

The Yankee boy's voice trailed off and he stood a moment, head down, thin hands gripping the edges of the pulpit.
It seemed that he must fall but he did not. Rather, he
raised his head again; and Buck could hear the sighing of
held breaths being released throughout the darkness beyond
the candle's shine.

"Finally Jesus said to the multitude that they were to
pray with him," the Yankee boy went on, "and that when
they did, they were to do it as he told them."

He bowed his head and Buck felt in the darkened pews
behind Mercer Barnes and himself the rustling stir of many
men doing the same thing. He looked over at his companion,
and the hard-faced Alabaman had his eyes cast down and
closed. Buck lowered his own gaze and the Yankee boy began the Lord's Prayer:

> "Our Father which art in heaven,
> Hallowed be thy name . . .
> For thine is the kingdom,
> And the power, and the glory,
> For ever. Amen."

This time there was no hiatus of silence when the Yankee
boy's voice faded. The amen was still on his slowing lips
when the front door of the church crashed inward.

The blaze of half a dozen unhooded bull's-eye lanterns
stabbed at the cowering soldiers in the bareboard pews,
and the voice of the Confederate lieutenant commanding Bragg's
police company broke coldly over their terror.

"You are under arrest. Any man moving to escape will be shot."

32   The Eighth Trooper

BUCK AND MERCER BARNES were standing in front of the pulpit, backs to the center aisle and the door. The instant Bragg's lieutenant shouted his order Barnes said out of the side of his mouth to Buck, "Red, I am going through that back window and you had better come along." The next moment he had barred his arms over his head and dived through the cobwebbed panes. Buck went after him unhesitatingly. They struck the ground outside and rolled to their feet to run squarely into the arms of a second police squad stationed at the rear of the church.

Two of the soldiers seized Barnes, who at once cried out for Buck to keep going. But Buck reached for J.C. Sutton's Navy Colt. The long barrel came down crackingly across the forehead of the nearest of Barnes' captors. The man dropped. Simultaneously, Barnes twisted free of the second trooper. He and Buck were running again. The latter leaped the fence around the church burial plot with ease, but Barnes caught a foot in the top pickets. He fell heavily back inside the plot. The remaining half-dozen Confederate troopers were upon him before he could rise and Buck was left with no choice. Wheeling, he threw the Colt's five shots into the massed group of the police squad. There was an instant melting of the mass, two high, almost womanish screams, a fractional wait, then a hoarse voice calling, "Jesus Christ, lay low—they have shot Billy Jack and old Jess!" Buck pulled Barnes to his feet and they ran on.

Over the ridge they circled back around to Church Road. There, at Barnes' insistence, they lay up in the dripping brush to wait for the police troops to come out of the church with the captured stragglers. They had heard a burst of rifle fire as they ran and Barnes had the idea their break might have inspired some of the others to try the side windows, or even rush the door.

"Sarge," said Buck, "you think I killed them two soldiers back there?"

Barnes shook his head. "Likely not," he said. "A man

don't cry out like that when he's centered. I'd say you
broke a shoulder, smashed a hip, splintered a leg maybe.
Them bone shots are the worst for pain. They bust you apart
with it."

"I pray to God they ain't dead. It was a vicious thing to
shoot blind into them like that. You think it was moral
wrong of me, Sarge?"

"What in the name of hell do you expect me to think?"
said Barnes quickly. "You saved my life with them shots.
You want me to argue morals with you?"

Buck frowned. "I don't see where I saved anybody's life,"
he said. "They wasn't shooting at us."

"No," rasped Barnes, "but Bragg's firing squad would have
been first thing in the morning."

"You're funning," said Buck. "Bragg nor nobody else
ain't going to shoot all them soldiers in that church."

Barnes looked at him. "We wasn't talking about *all them
soldiers*, Red," he said. "We was talking about me and you.
If they stood fast, they won't be facing nothing worse than
twenty lashes. But me and you, we jumped a direct order
of arrest." He paused, shaking his head somberly. "Red," he
said, "once we dove through that window we wasn't running
for the skins of our backs, we was running for our lives."

"I don't believe it," said Buck stubbornly. "We should have
stayed and took our medicine. God, I hope them boys wasn't
bad hurt. I pray to Jesus they wasn't."

"Praying won't change nothing but your standing in
church," said Barnes.

Buck, angered and casting about for some way to get
back at the Alabaman, suddenly remembered something odd
he had noted when the candle was lit in the church.

"Say," he challenged stiffly, "whatever happened to Lieutenant Mercer Barnes?"

"Who?"

"You know who!" snorted Buck in triumph. "What did
you do? Take off that lieutenant's coat so you could sprint
faster?"

"You might say so," Barnes admitted. "Do you remember
what we did *not* see when we looked at all them stragglers
huddled in the dark?"

"No, what?"

"We did not see no officers, that's what."

"So?" prompted Buck.

"I mean to say those soldiers would have knocked my
head in if they had seen that coat on me. I mean to say

that's why I peeled it off and stuffed it down behind that rear pew before your matchlight got out of their eyes."

"You being an officer is what made you stampede out the window, too, I guess."

Barnes nodded grimly.

"Yeah," he said. "And you being Bragg's personal courier put you alongside of me in more of a way than just standing there in front of that damned pulpit, Red, and don't you forget it. It's why I give you the word to come along. Now you got any more moral or military doubts you want straightened out before I drown?"

"No, sir," said Buck, and fell still.

Barnes, after a long minute of watching down the road, said warningly, "Meeting's breaking up yonder. Now we'll know."

First out of the church were two troopers with lanterns. They flanked the door, throwing their lights across it. Then came the lieutenant and the company sergeant, also and in turn standing aside. Next a small knot of prisoners—no more than seven or eight—marched out, followed by a file of guards, muskets at the ready.

"Damn," breathed Mercer Barnes. "Just what I feared. The whole bunch broke after we did. That was the rifle fire we heard, all right."

"Oh, Lord," groaned Buck. "You figure them few boys coming out was all that was left able to walk?"

Barnes watched the police squad march to the road, come slogging up the rise.

"Not likely, Red," he said. "I figure most of the other boys made it safe away, same as we did. Not all of them, though. There's lights still in the church. That means there's wounded in there. Dead, too, possibly."

Buck shuddered. "I hope to God them boys I hit ain't among them," he said. "The dead ones, that is."

"If they are," said Barnes, "they ain't no worse off than those poor bastards coming our way up the hill. They didn't know they was going to get shot. These here boys do."

Buck lay watching the doomed men draw near.

"Bragg," Barnes said with bitter softness, "will have those boys shot the first chance he gets. They're as good as dead where they stand, the whole eight of them."

"Eight?" said Buck. "I thought I counted seven."

"Count again," said Mercer Barnes.

Buck did. There were eight of the condemned troopers.

Buck's heart grew stone cold within him. The eighth trooper was Miller Nalls.

33   The Pay of Heroes

BUCK AND MERCER BARNES, circling through the rain-lashed wood to avoid Bragg's police squadrons, found a haven of anonymity among the mixed thousands of troops surrounding Beauregard's Confederate headquarters on Sherman's camp-ground adjacent to Shiloh Church. His abandoned camp was a military bonanza. The starving, undershirtless, even shoeless recruits of the butternut gray were denying themselves nothing of this spectacular prize. Their officers, perhaps advisedly, made no effort to check or even to supervise the rape of the Federal supply dumps.

At ten minutes after one a scout came in to Beauregard's aide with the first of five ominous reports, but Beauregard was enjoying his sleep in Sherman's bed. He would not leave it. At 4:00 A.M. Beauregard was advised that U.S. Grant had twenty-three thousand new troops on the ground. It was time to get up.

Beauregard was not long with his decision. While not considering his position desperate, neither did he mean to contend seriously with Grant for anything more than the necessary time to make his withdrawal toward Corinth an orderly one. To cover that intention he must stage a convincing forenoon resistance. And to underwrite that resistance he must arrange the best possible rearguard delay. He well knew where to purchase this item at the lowest price. It was fifteen minutes after four in the morning when he sent for Braxton Bragg.

From dawn until all danger of a Southern break was past at 2:00 P.M.—the hour at which Beauregard issued the official order to leave the field—Bragg hung like grim death to the shell-torn reaches of Shiloh Wood, repeatedly driving in the probes of Lew Wallace at his center, the pawings of Sherman and Buell at his flanks. It was one of the great rearguard classics of the war. Through it, with some six thousand ambulatory wounded and half-mutinous men, Bragg staved off the assault of fifty thousand Union troops for nine hours.

Buck Burnet was one of Bragg's walking cripples. He received the wound as a reward for an unwarranted foolishness in which he, Mercer Barnes, Tellis Yeager and five fellow Confederate volunteers rushed a two-gun battery of Union six-pounders on a rise which commanded the center-field gully where the Southern retreat must cross.

When the rejoined comrades reached this position, unheroically in the lead of the Florida Corps retirement, the Federal guns had just gone into action. Now, as they crouched in the brush at gully's edge, the six-pounders were rattling mixed salvos of grape, solid ball and double canister down the narrow depression like bursts of buckshot through a smoothbore gunbarrel. To cross in face of this fire meant another Hornet's Nest. To turn riverward for a lower crossing would be to come under the muzzles of Foote's gunboats, an equal disaster. The choice of moves was a difficult one for Bragg, with surrender at discretion being the reasonable option.

While the Confederate rearguard commander hesitated over this unfair trick of tactical luck, Brevet-Lieutenant Mercer Barnes did not. Turning to his companions he said calmly, "Boys, I think we can flank them guns."

"Grab him!" said Tellis Yeager. "He's gone off his head!"

Buck said, "Sarge, I got to agree. You couldn't take them guns with a brigade."

"No," said Barnes, "but you might with a squad."

While Buck and Tellis dropped their mouths, Barnes turned to the ragged audience which had drifted up.

"What do you say, men?" he asked. "Who's game to go up the gully with me and cut down them Yankee gun crews before the Feds can get troops up there to support them? Speak up, men!"

There were upwards of two hundred Confederate soldiers within range. Not one of them moved. Then Tellis Yeager shook his head doubtfully.

"Well," he said, "I ain't exactly no hero, but these here Union shoes I requisitioned last night are killing me. I got to exchange them for a bigger pair or go barefoot again."

With the words he moved to Barnes' side. Buck Burnet was one step behind him. Again silence. Then a gaunt man with gray hair and empty eyes limped out. "I lost two kid brothers yesterday," he said.

A hulking bear of a fellow followed him. "I got me a slick-legged widow waiting in Corinth," he growled. "Told her I'd be back inside three days. Ain't no damn Yank artillery going to make a liar out of Mapes Tolliver."

"If that's the same widow woman I got waiting for me,"
drawled a lanky Georgia cracker, "I will surrender you my
share of her and welcome to the itch."

This drew its rough laugh but neither the Georgia man
nor any of his appreciators offered to testify further. In
nearly ten minutes of talking Barnes obtained but four more
volunteers. Barnes now spoke with scathing gentleness.

"If we get the guns," he said, "we'll wave a shirt from up
yonder on the hill. Meanwhile, would it be asking too much
of you patriots to pass on the good word to the General?
There won't be no time for us to spike them pieces, so he
will have to get some troops up there in a hurry to hold off
the Feds till they can be hooked up and hauled out. What
you say?"

"You wave the shirt, Alabam," one said, "we'll see Bragg
gets the word. But you're a damn fool regardless."

"Come on, boys," Barnes said. "Half of you with me,
half with Red, yonder. My bunch will take the far gun,
Red's the near. Keep as still as you can, move fast, pray
hard." He looked a moment at Buck. "Good-bye, Red," he
said. "Watch yourself."

Ten minutes later they had got behind and rushed the
Union guns.

It was a brief, brutal business ending with the Yankee
artillery crews shot or clubbed down to the man, and with
five of the seven Confederates who had destroyed them
lying with them in the trampled earth about the carriages of
the silenced cannon. Only Buck and Tellis Yeager were
still standing, and Tellis had to wave the signal shirt to the
waiting group below. Buck had taken a fifty caliber Springfield ball through his left arm high and inside at the shoulder, shattering the bone and sickening him with such pain
that he could remain upright only by clutching at the near
wheel of the number-one gun with his good arm. Across
the taildrag of the other piece Mercer Barnes lay dying.
When he could, Buck staggered to him. He crouched in
the dirt with his head in his lap, holding him close, crooning
and mumbling over him in a blank-faced, tearless way. When
Tellis came over to crouch with them, he was too late.
Barnes had died so quietly the dazed Texas youth did not
know he had slipped away until Tellis reached over and
took him firmly by the shoulder and said, "Put him down,
kid, he's gone."

They sat there for a wordless spell after that. Down below
they could hear the Southern troopers breaking out of the

woods to come up the hill and make good the capture of the Union guns. Buck roused himself and said to Tellis, "Will you give me a hand up, please? I should like to be standing when they get here." Tellis nodded and helped him to rise. Limping to the front of the knoll they could see the first tide of Bragg's released army flooding across the gully. The men were shouting at one another in a quick return of spirit. Buck and Tellis exchanged nodding glances and turned to look for a last, white-lipped time at the lifeless body of their friend Mercer Barnes.

"You remember," said Tellis bitterly, "what he always used to say about how being a hero paid so poor? He was sure as son of a bitching right, wasn't he?"

Buck did not reply at once but turned for a moment to watch the continuing crossing of the rescued Confederate troops below. Presently he shook his head.

"No," he answered, still staring below, "he was wrong. It pays pretty good."

It was general knowledge Monday morning that some soldiers had been caught hiding in Shiloh Church Sunday night. The rumor then spread early Monday afternoon that Bragg was not going to treat these men as stragglers (fifteen to twenty lashes before their companies), or even as having been absent without leave (thirty-nine lashes in public assembly of all troops), but was going to charge them with desertion and have them shot that same sundown. Buck Burnet himself did not make it through to that day's end, so could not know if the rumor were true. It was four o'clock in the afternoon of April 7th when he stumbled and went down into the red clay of the Corinth road. It was early evening of the twenty-ninth of May—seven weeks later —when conscious memory came back and he sat bolt upright on a filthy hospital cot, eyes wide in groping dismay.

He saw before him a long, dimly lit hallway. It was narrow, musty-odored, many-doored, villainously carpeted; and he knew it for a hotel corridor though he had never seen one. Lining it, banked as thickly as the tiers of dead stacked along the sunken road at Shiloh, were facing double rows of unspeakably dirty cots and fetid wounded. Beyond the cots, at the corridor's end, a paneless window framed listless patterns of sycamores against the humid twilight. Buck spoke haltingly to the fine-looking woman bending over him.

"Please, ma'am, what place is this?" he asked. "Am I a prisoner here?"

"No, soldier, you're a patient." The tall woman smiled

down at him. "I'm your nurse and this is the Tishomingo Hotel hospital in Corinth."

Buck nodded frowningly. "The Confederates are still here then, ma'am?" he said presently.

"What's left of them, yes. How do you feel, soldier?"

"Peaked, ma'am. How long have I been here?"

"You wouldn't believe how long. Your wound has been healed some little time, and you've been up and around the past few days. It's your mind that's been refusing to come back. You'll be just fine now. What's your name, soldier?"

"Buck Burnet, ma'am. Might I ask yours?"

"Ella Newsome," she nodded. "Where you from, Buck Burnet?"

"Texas, ma'am. Concho County, south of the river. I joined up at Marion Junction, Mississippi, though. The Pensacola Light Blues. They was a Florida regiment with Bragg. Ain't many left of them. Maybe none at all other than me."

"*You* shouldn't be. No man was ever luckier to be alive." Ella Newsome straightened, added briskly, "Get up now. We're going down to see Miss Kate. That is, if you're up to it."

Buck winced, moved one leg gingerly.

"I reckon I might take a set at it," he answered. With a hard clenching of the teeth, he made it to his feet. After a shaky moment, he grinned palely. "By the right flank march, ma'am?"

She stepped in quickly to support him. "By the right flank march!" she smiled. "Here, put your good arm around my shoulder."

Buck stopped midway in his hopeful stride to meet her. He kept his eyes level with hers. Instinctively, he tried the right arm first. It responded by moving upward into view. When he tried the left arm the sensation of responding movement was equally strong but nothing rose into his line of vision. Still he did not look down. Neither did he curse nor cry out. But the glance he shot Ella Newsome was more eloquent than any profanity, the question in it more plaintive than any outcry. She nodded gravely.

"Yes, soldier," she said, "it's gone."

Buck searched her face a long, still moment. Then he nodded in quiet turn and said, "Thank you, ma'am, thank you very much," and put his arm about her shoulder and went with her down the dark hallway toward the dim light at its far end.

34   Tishomingo Hotel

AN HOUR LATER Buck walked out of the Tishomingo Hotel hospital into the oppressive quiet of the May night. It was only a little after 7:00 P.M. but the town lay still as a new corpse. Buck knew why, and he sat down on the veranda steps to think about it. He chose a place where the shadows of the sycamores were deep, and where one of the columns hid him. He had seen himself in a cracked wall mirror in the hall ward upstairs, and did not want others to share the experience. Neither did he want his brief hour of final decision interrupted. He had to be right about what he did now. A hard way lay behind him, and an even harder way stretched ahead. And his time was limited to the coming sunrise. This was a military, not a personal condition. The Union general "Old Brains" Halleck and one hundred twenty-five thousand men lay just outside the city. Corinth would be occupied by the blue enemy with first daylight tomorrow.

Eleven hours, less than eleven hours, thought Buck.

It did not leave a man much room. Should he stay here at Tishomingo with the abandoned hopeless of the Shiloh wounded, or should he struggle on toward Tupelo and the reëstablishing Confederate line, fifty miles southward?

That was the choice now. The only military units left inside the city were Bragg's omnipresent floating squads ranging the back alleys to do the last dirty cleaning up. Buck shook his head, pondering heavily on this fact, as well as upon the rest of the information he had gained from the hospital orderlies and fellow patients. A very great deal had happened during his seven weeks away from the fighting. The military details leading to Beauregard's scuttling retreat to Tupelo were made very clear to Buck. It was only when he came to inquire on the personal level that he drew blank looks, or abrupt answers. What executions were those about which he asked? Eight men shot for desertion? By Braxton Bragg at sundown of the seventh? What is that you say? On the road back from Shiloh! Dear Lord, man, that was *April* 7th! Nearly sixty days ago! Buck knew then what had happened, or suspected that he did.

The end of Miller Nalls and the Shiloh Church skulkers

belonged to a much smaller history than that dangerous one now encircling Corinth, Mississippi. Their fate mattered nothing at all now. No one could remember it, or wanted to remember it. Still a man tried his best to uncover some shadow of a trial.

There had been, actually, one pertinent suggestion from a one-legged corporal of North Carolina volunteers. This man pointed out that the office of the Provost Marshal was still open down at the depot, and that if Buck himself were not wanted for desertion, or worse, he might go down there to inquire after his friends who were, or anyway had been, so wanted.

Buck shook his head once more and peered through the deepening night toward the deserted main street. Far down it, toward the tracks, he could see the faint glow of the oil lamp in the window of the Provost Marshal's office.

It appeared to be fifty miles just down to the station. But either he went down there and did what he could about getting out of Corinth, or he waited where he was, certain, alike, of the coming sunrise and of the good Yankee food and skilled medical care which would come with that sunrise. This was the question, then, very simply.

Presently he stood up. He weaved unsteadily, braced himself for a moment's recovery against the veranda's column. Then he went on across the lawn to the street, toward the depot.

There was a lone trooper on duty outside the door of the Provost Marshal's office. Buck's heart picked up at the sight of his homely, slab-sided silhouette against the lamplight. It was Tellis Yeager. Buck came up quiet as an Indian.

" 'Tenshun!" Buck snapped. Then, as Yeager hit into a guilty brace, "Give the challenge of the night, Sergeant!"

Yeager, looking straight ahead, answered stiffly. "All leaves are green in May, sir. Give the counterchallenge."

"Artillery Hill," said Buck, and Yeager spun about crying, "Red! God bless my soul, we heard you'd dropped dead on the road back. Where you been hiding at?"

"Yonder at Tishomingo Hotel with the rest of Beauregard's blunders."

"Oh, yeah, I see." The other soldier eyed him. "It's hell about your arm, Red. I didn't notice right off."

"I didn't mean for you to," replied Buck. "I reckon, though, that it's still fresh enough for me to be feeling sorry for myself."

"Hell, you got a right. That's a terrible thing, to lose an arm."

"It's worse to lose a friend," said Buck.

"Yeah. I allow you mean like old Mercer."

"Or like Miller Nalls."

"Nalls? Why him?"

"Tellis," said Buck, "when a man is your best friend it don't make no difference whether he dies gallant or is shot down like a yeller dawg for desertion. It's the same hurt to you; he's still dead and gone."

"Boy," said Yeager, "Nalls ain't dead. He's sure as hell gone, though. Got clean away."

"Thank God," said Buck, sinking weakly to the paintless planks of the depot bench. "Oh, thank God it's so."

"Maybe, maybe not. He's as good as dead regardless. He kilt two guards getting away. There's been a conscription act passed since you been sick. They done changed our one-year enlistments to 'duration of the war.' Desertion's the thing this spring. Bragg is blowing up a fuss fit to end up half the army in front of the firing squad. You can bet your life he will get that mulehead Nalls. And when he does he will draw up the whole damned Army of the Mississippi to see the boy shot."

Buck said numbly, "Yes, I suppose he might. Providing it was his army to draw up, that is."

"It *will* be his army," said Yeager. "Beauregard is going to quit when he gets to Tupelo. He's sick."

"What's that to do with Bragg?"

"Bragg's getting the command. And I mean of the whole damned army out here."

"I'm glad," said Buck. "That damned Beauregard cost us Shiloh. Bragg could have beat Grant up there. Give the chance he'll still do it. Further, he ain't half the monster he's made out. He treated me square, and will again, I vow."

"You mean to tell me you're going to see him about new duty? With that arm gone?"

"With the arm gone there ain't no other way I could get assigned."

"Yeah, I reckon that's so. But I can't understand you, Red. Why don't you quit and go home while you can? Cut on down the road past Tupelo and hit for Texas. God, boy, I wisht I could go home."

He broke off, looking away.

"Tellis," said Buck softly, "you didn't finish telling me about Miller getting away."

"Yeah, well it was strange, Red. It was him being so big and gentle and friendly and soft in his ways that fooled them, you see. But Lord God, he turned into a tiger right there in the Corinth road.

"It was along about five o'clock in a bad part of the woods. The prisoner detail had straggled some and was separated from the next troops by the bend in the road. Just as they march into this bend, here comes a runner from Bragg. The word is to get a hustle on and bring up them deserters to column head. Bragg is going to pull up and have them shot at six o'clock sundown.

"Well sir, Nalls just sets his heels in the dirt and says real quiet, 'No he ain't. We wasn't doing nothing wrong in that church. Only resting some and maybe praying a little. It ain't right to shoot a man for something he ain't done and didn't even have in his heart and mind to do.'

"My friend the squad corporal says that he is sorry about the order but that he would have to obey it.

"Nalls says, 'Don't nobody stand in my way, please, for I am going out of here and don't want to hurt nobody on my way.'

"Well, my friend drops his mouth open to say something but he don't never get it out. Nalls comes out from under his shirt with a rock big as a rattlesnake melon and flings this boulder square into his belly. Knocked him ten feet into a stump and out of the fight.

"Now them prisoners was in leg irons only. So each of them grabbed for the guard nearest him. Before a shot could be triggered off, the prisoners had the guns and the guards were standing there stupid as jaybirds.

"Nalls then says, 'Please don't none of you try nothing, you done your best.' Then he gets the leg-iron keys off the corporal and they get set to take off. It was then that two of them six guards made a damn-fool dive to get their guns back. Nalls picks up a three-foot length of leg-chain with the iron cuff on it. He hit the first guard in the back of the neck and cut his spine through. The second guard got the ankle cuff acrost the eyes. They say his skull popped open like somebody had stepped on a rotten yard-egg. My friend said it put the fear of God into him and the other guards. They just stood there and watched the prisoners go diving into the swamp."

"God damn them," said Buck. "They drove him to it. The sons of bitches pushed the poor dumb thing to where he went crazy—to where he didn't have no human sense at all left in him."

"No, Red," said Tellis Yeager soberly, "it wasn't *them* drove him to it. It was your friend the General. Jesus Christ, boy, ain't you ready to see that yet? It was Bragg, you hear?"

Buck Burnet said nothing. But at last the black anger was rising in him. His hand dropped unconsciously to the handle of J.C. Sutton's Navy Colt—the only friend he had left now —and the taint of murder was in him. "Maybe," said Buck, still deadly quiet, "I been wrong about him. Did they catch any of the other poor fellers yet?"

"Three of them. They was shot on sight. Five, including your friend, are still loose and have likely made it to the Yankee lines. But I wouldn't bet on it. Bragg has had his own men and all the Provost Marshal could spare hunting them around the clock. He's even took Wirt Rambeau off staff duty and put him to leading a police squad. Matter of fact he's down south of town this minute running out a report. Corporal Craney just rode in for some more men to go down and help Rambeau's bunch. He's inside there with Major Shelby now. Seems they got a tip from a farmer says he seen two soldiers hiding out in a old barn on his back piece. One of them was a big devil. Says he took a shot at them. Hit one of them, he thinks."

"Where was all this, Tellis?"

"Rainy Crick. Place about five mile south on the Tupelo road. Dade Youngerford's Hundred. There's a cowpath crossroads sign at the cutoff. Farmer said he'd have a barn lantern hung on it."

Buck took a deep, slow breath and stood up. For the first time he saw the way ahead. It gave him strength. It let him know why the Lord had saved him at Shiloh Church, The Hornet's Nest, Artillery Hill and Tishomingo Hotel. He moved toward Tellis Yeager pointing to a strawberry roan pony at the depot hitching rail, one of the Texas remounts from Bragg's picket.

"Is that Craney's horse yonder?" he asked.

"It is," answered Yeager, watching him.

"He's from my string. I remember him. Got a hard mouth but a long mover. I picked him for a doer."

Yeager was still watching him. "You got a good memory for a horse, Red," he said warningly. "Let's leave it go at that."

"What you saying, Tellis?"

"I'm on duty; don't try nothing."

"He's a powerful good horse," said Buck. "But I reckon you got me wrong. Thank you for everything, Tellis, and remember me to Corporal Craney. He done me a good turn once. Oh, say, ain't that Craney coming out now . . .?"

The ruse caught Yeager. He half turned toward the office door. The barrel of the Navy Colt cracked across his head as he tried to check his turn and swing back on Buck. Buck grabbed him as he fell, propped him up on the depot bench, put his hat back on and his rifle carefully across his lap. Then he slid past the lamplight coming from the depot window and went for the roan pony. It was touchy work getting up on him with one hand but the pony winded him with a remembering whicker and stood steady as a buggy mare to his fumbling mount. It was well he did. Behind him Buck heard the office door bang open.

He pulled the roan free of the rail just as Craney came around the corner of the building and saw him. Bragg's corporal planted his feet and started blasting with a huge revolver. Terrified, the range pony squatted, squalled, came unbunched and lit out on a flat-bellied run. In thirty pounding jumps he had Buck Burnet safely away and hammering down the blind dark of the Tupelo road.

35 Youngerford's Hundred

ONCE AWAY, Buck pulled in the roan. The little mustang had a natural singlefoot and Buck let him take it. The washy feeling in Buck's stomach told him that if he did not go conservatively at the start, he would not go any gait at the finish. Fortunately Craney had ridden with knotted reins, letting Buck drop them without losing them. Thus freed, his hand could grip the saddlehorn. He was beginning to realize what he had done at the depot.

He was now as much a fugitive as Miller Nalls. When Yeager woke up he would have to add his story to Craney's. For either soldier to hide Buck's identity would be to risk putting his neck where Buck's and Miller's were. Buck tightened his wasted hand on the saddlehorn, peered hard ahead.

It was an oppressive night, even for lowland Mississippi. A muggy swathing of bottomland mist hugged the Corinth countryside. The sound of a shod hoof in the spongy dirt of the roadway was blotted up within a pebble's toss. Off to the west heat lightning simmered sporadically. To the east the darkness was blue-black. Behind him Buck could hear no sound of Craney and the Provost Marshal's men. Ahead he could see no sign of Wirt Rambeau and Bragg's squad. It was a blind, bad situation.

In the fog beyond the roan's nose he heard the sudden muted jingle of a bit chain. Then a man's deep cough, raw with weather.

He saw his pony's ears flick and set forward. He put his hand along his neck, finding and holding his velvety muzzle. *"Hoh, shuh,"* he whispered, "be still," and steadied him with a slow pressure of both knees against his tensing sides.

The roan hesitated but he was bunching to run. Damn, thought Buck, that would be Wirt Rambeau and his squad. He had begun to hope he had headed them. Now it was ride through them or quit. At the thought, the idea came to him. He was riding Craney's horse. Craney was a staff courier for Bragg. Bragg was in Tupelo.

The roan was squatting like a rabbit now, would go any instant with or without his rider. *"Hee-yahh!"* yelled Buck, and let go of his muzzle. In the same breath he shouted, "Roadway! Roadway! Courier for Tupelo!" and set himself for the headlong crash through the horses ahead. The roan steered through the scattering cavalry mounts with no more than a shoulder bump, a rump scrape, and some assorted, outraged countershouts from the cursing soldiers. But Buck had heard what he wanted to hear before the second thoughts of profanity had been employed. "Say," cried one sharp-eyed trooper, "that was Craney's horse! Hey, Craney! Where the hell's the fire?" And, from a fellow squadsman, fading out beneath the drum of the roan's hooves and the resettling swirl of the disturbed fog, "Jesus Gawd A'mighty, what a life! Even the yeller dawgs step on you since Shiloh!"

Safely past them Buck slowed the roan to his singlefoot. His grin was white and beaded with perspiration but it was a grin. "Yeller dawgs" was the Rebel infantryman's name for the horse-mounted couriers. Buck knew he had won his gamble; he was past them and they had, indeed, taken him for Staff Corporal Craney riding hell-for-leather to reach Bragg at Tupelo. The advantage, however, would last exactly as long as it took the real Craney to catch up with Sergeant Wirt Rambeau's man hunters.

He was on top of the cowpath crossing before he could get the roan stopped. Wheeling quickly, he brought the nervous little horse back toward the ringy halo of lantern light which had bloomed without warning on his right. As he did, he heard the ferocious baying of hounds through the intervening fog. Next moment he was looking down on a pale-eyed man in the shapeless rags of a sharecropping farmer.

The man had a wolf tooth which he displayed in an unmoving grimace of suspicion and distrust. His face was dirtied with a gray stubble of week-old whisker laced with dried egg and tobacco dribble. He had no shoes upon his feet, held a big-bore "Old Reliable" model Sharps Rifle in his right hand and, in his left, the leash chains of three crossbred hounds. Above his head, floating in the fog, was a gray pine board bearing the legend: Youngerford's Hundred.

"You Dade Youngerford?" Buck asked carefully.

When he spoke the hounds broke into renewed lunging to get at him, and the mustang pony shied wildly. Their owner lifted his lip over the wolf tooth. "Reckon I know who I am," he lisped. "Question is, who are you?"

"I'm from the Provost Marshal's office up to Corinth. Got a sergeant and ten men following behind me. We had a complaint from a Dade Youngerford on Rainy Crick about two deserters hiding out on his place."

"Made the complaint myself," nodded the man. "Question is, where's your sergeant and his ten men?"

"Right behind me like I said. I was out front to make sure we didn't miss the turn-off."

"Well you didn't, did you? Question now is, are you really from the Provost Marshal's office?"

Buck was having all he could do to hold the roan in and said angrily, "You quiet them dawgs down, mister, or I will ride them over. This horse ain't broke to stand to that kind of upset, you hear?"

"I know he ain't," leered the man.

Buck felt his hackles rise. "How's that?" he queried.

"He goosed the same way when the other feller was on him," said the sharecropper. "The one I talked to about them damned deserters in my barn."

"You *are* Dade Youngerford," challenged Buck scowlingly. The other nodded, shifted his Sharps upward.

"Question still is," he said, "who are you?"

"I done told you. The sergeant said you'd be here at the signpost to guide us in."

"Now that," drawled the yellow-eyed sharecropper, "is downright remarkable. Seeing's how."

Buck tensed. "Seeing's how what?" he asked.

"Seeing's how I never said no such thing."

Caught in the slip, feeling weak and sick from the ride and the frustration of this last-minute cruelty, Buck almost gave in. Then his black anger came back to give him strength once more.

"Well now I reckon," he said, "That we had better wait up right here and see what the sergeant has to say about that."

"Yes," agreed the ragged tenant, exposing his wolf tooth full length. "I reckon we had best do just that. There ain't no shiftless, one-armed, mustered-out soldier going to do me out of my report money."

"Do you out of your *what?*" Buck asked unbelievingly.

"Report money!" snarled the other. "You know well as I do Bragg's paying a dollar a head for deserters."

"*A dollar a head,*" whispered Buck Burnet. "My God . . ."

He sat looking down at the man. And he knew of a sudden what it was he must do about Dade Youngerford and his old, abandoned ratbin of a barn.

"These boys ain't the first you've caught with the bait of that old barn, are they?" he asked. "I'll warrant you've made more out of that barn since Shiloh than you've cropped off this hundred since you've been on it."

"It's an honest man's place to report those . . ." the wolf-toothed man began guiltily, then stopped with an ugly growl. "Now you hesh up your dirty mouth, goddam you!" he said. "I don't need to answer to such as you. Not for nothing. You might even be worth a dollar yourself." He jabbed the Sharps at Buck. "Now you just hold that boogery horse right where he is till them Provost Marshal's men get here. By God, we'll just see about you when they show up."

Buck smiled wanly, shook his head.

"No," he said quietly, "I reckon we'll see about me right now, Mr. Youngerford."

The sneering bounty hunter did not see the movement of the hand which killed him. He saw only the burst of orange fire which seared his face, point-blank. His finger spasmed shut on the trigger of his Sharps and the big rifle flamed back at the tall boy on the roan pony in the same moment that he fell dead atop his yammering dogs, trapping the brutes in the tangle of their own chains. Buck, reeling under the impact of the blunt-nosed Sharps slug, rose in his stirrups and fired straight down into the imprisoned animals—one, two, three deliberate times. The roan squealed in panic, gathering himself to leap away from the bloody dogs and the bombarding gunfire. Buck threw the last, fifth shot, at the lantern. It crashed out and the roan bolted westward, away from the Tupelo road, racing down the fog-choked wagon track toward Youngerford's Hundred.

36   The Road to Tupelo

THE FOG WAS HEAVIER in the Rainy Creek bottoms than it had been on the Tupelo road. Buck had to cast out in circles from the farmhouse to be certain he would not miss the rickety barn. He was lucky, coming upon it with the third cast. His face was now white as bleached clay. His fist clawed the saddlehorn like the talons of a stricken bird. Yet there was no time for rest. Bragg's troopers would soon find the signpost with the grisly token Buck had left lying at its foot. When they did that their pace would change.

Rambeau had surely been hanging back in his approach to the Youngerford place. Buck remembered that the old soldier had a son nearly his own age. He could imagine Rambeau's feelings about being transferred to police work where his main duty was to ferret out fugitive, frightened boys and turn them over to the mercies of Bragg's firing squads. Yet he knew the Rambeau who had insisted he write a letter home to his grandparents the night before Shiloh and the Rambeau who would shortly be coming down the Youngerford wagon track were two different staff sergeants. The business of taking two starving, helpless youths cornered in a sagging old bat-cave of a barn, was one thing. That of coming in on two deserters who had trailed up and killed in cold blood a tenant farmer and his three dogs, was another. And there could be no doubt that Rambeau and his men would credit the signpost massacre to Miller and his companion.

Buck shook himself. Lord, God, he was weary. He must get Miller aroused and away from there. He must hurry.

"Miller, you in there? It's me, Buck."

Buck shivered with weakness.

"Miller!" he called sharply.

"Buck . . ." The familiar slow voice answered with his name, then broke and fell still and Buck could get no second response when he called again.

"Miller," he called, "I'm coming in there. Now don't shoot, it's only me, Buck. I got a good horse and there's two mules up to the front shed. We got to gather up and get shut of here. Rambeau's right behind me. Craney's following him with a Provost Marshal's detail. But we got time, boy, we got time . . ." He talked as he moved forward, knowing how hunted things will act when worn crazy from being chased and hounded and shot at day and night. When any living thing had been run like those poor boys in the barn they would as soon shoot their dearest friend as most savage enemy. So Buck, sick and shaky as he was himself, talked his way warily until he was five careful steps into the barn. Then he stopped dead and called out uncertainly.

"Miller?"

His answer, as before, was creeping silence.

"Miller!" he croaked.

"Buck, old Buck . . ." The whisper was thin, reedy, full of effort, and it frightened Buck.

"Where you at, Miller?" he said.

"Here, Buck. Over past the partition inside the door."

The other boy's voice stopped again, scarily, and Buck said quickly, "All right, Miller, I'm coming. Keep talking so's I can follow your voice."

He looped the pony's reins over his arm, starting toward the last sound of his friend's voice. But the latter was no longer talking and he had to find him by feeling with his foot along the floor. When he came to him in this cray-fishing way he knelt, reaching blindly. He touched his body. His hand came away wet, warm and sticky. The roan got the rank smell of the blood in his nostrils and sprang back in alarm. He dragged Buck ten feet, crashing him into the partition and stunning him. When he could, Buck lurched to his feet.

He got the roan quieted and tied to an ancient manger, then started out to find Miller again. His reaching foot struck nothing, plunged into a deep hole in the broken floor-ing, threw him headlong. This time he could not get up and made the remainder of the way to Miller crawling on hands and knees. It seemed to take him half an hour. When he had completed the journey his vision had adjusted to the deep gloom. He now saw Miller's wasted body, back flat, on a shucking of mildewed hay beside an old hasp-lidded oatbin. He could see the rise and fall of his sunken chest and hear the raking labor of his breathing.

Wondering if Miller had his eyes open and could see him, too, he decided that he might. Accordingly, he forced him-self up against the side of the oatbin.

"Miller," he asked softly, "you hear me?"

"Sure, sure, Buck. When did you get here? Where you been all this time?"

Buck wet his compressed lips.

"Miller," he said, "how bad you hit?"

There was a stretching silence, then Miller said, "I won't be going home with you, Buck. But, oh, you will never know how sweet it is to hear your voice again. To know you're here and are all right. Old Buck. Good old Buck Burnet."

Buck reached for his hand. It was cold as waterhole ice in October. He remembered then where he had touched him when the mustang spooked and he said, "You hit in the belly, Miller?"

He could see the big round head move in denial.

"No, that's where it come out, Buck. Went clear through back to front. It was an old Sharps. I could tell by the sound."

Buck squeezed and patted his hand.

"Does it still hurt you terrible bad?"

"No. It like to killed me at first, but now I don't really feel nothing but a sort of froze cold. Simms he said it left a whopper of a hole."

"Was Simms the boy with you?"

"Yep. Simms Renfro. He's gone on acrost the crick like I told him. We both knowed I was gone up the flue and he was sensible about it. Most would have wanted to auger it but Simms he knew."

"Listen," said Buck, "he didn't know nothing. You're going to make it, you hear? Soon as I rest a bit, I'm going back up to the front shed and fetch one of them mules down here for you. We'll make it away together, you hear me, Miller? I brung you to this here dance and I'm agoing to take you home from it."

"Buck, you know better than that." The round head wagged again. "You get out of here. Shag on acrost the crick. Head for home. Jesus, don't you think a man knows when his insides is all bled out of him?"

"Shut up, Miller, shut up."

"When you get there, Buck, say hello to Grandpa and Grandma Burnet for me. Tell them I made it to the war and done well in it. And say, Willy Bill said he would wait at the river, remember? So if you should see him at Paint Rock Crossing you tell him I will be along directly. I reckon I got to go look for Eubie and Little Bit and old Todo before I start back, and that might take some little time. But I'll be along."

He was suddenly lucid again, his hand searching for Buck's in the darkness.

"Now, Buck, it's only a hundred miles to the big river, and that Texas pony will get you there in two nights easy. Now you do it, you hear, Buck. You do it for me. Go home, Buck, go home . . ."

Buck reached out and put his fingers to the other boy's lips. There was a great weariness in his own voice, a resignation almost as great as that in his friend's, but there was no defeat in it, and no fear.

"Miller," he said, "I ain't going no place without you. We will wait here and rest a bit, then I will go and fetch that mule for you. We will hit for the Mississippi like you say, traveling nights and keeping to the brush days. We will make it to the Red, Miller, and we will make it to Caddo Swamp and on home to the Concho. But we will make it together, all the way, like always."

He used his last strength to gather the dying boy's head in the comfort of his arm, holding him close.

"Rest easy," he said, "we will go on directly."

Miller let his shaggy head ease down.

"Buck," he sighed, "I am grateful to you. It was terrible lonesome before you got here." Then, his voice taking on the curious detachment from main thoughts so typical of the traveler who knows he will not return, "Buck, where at you been all this time, you rascal? I been telling Simms you would show up every day for seems like a year. Where you been, Buck?"

"In the hospital at Corinth. I took one in the arm at the gully on the way back."

"That gully was pure hell, wasn't it, Buck? That's where I lost Eubie. One minute he was yelling and whooping square alongside me. Next thing I look around he ain't there. He just ain't there."

"I know, I know, Miller."

"You all better now, Buck?"

"All better, Miller."

The mustang threw up his head in the stall and cleared his nostrils with the peculiar snuffling snort so familiar to the prairie boys. This time, however, he did not whicker aloud but made a low chuckling noise in his throat.

"He winds something," said Buck. "Maybe them mules."

He felt his friend's head move against his chest.

"No, that ain't a smelling noise he made, Buck. You know that. He heard something. Likely them fellers coming for me."

Buck patted Miller's shoulder and murmured quietingly, "No, it ain't them fellers. They wasn't that close to me."

Miller let it pass.

"Buck," he said.

"Yes."

"We ain't going to make it to Richmond, are we?"

"I reckon not this trip."

"Buck, you blame me for what I done? Breaking away from them fellers what was going to shoot me?"

"Never."

"That's good. I was afeared you might. But it didn't seem rightly fair they was going to shoot me for something so small and mean. It still ain't clear in my mind what it was I done wrong. Can you tell me that, Buck? What it was I done that deserved killing?"

"No," said Buck. "Not me, nor nobody, can tell you that. There ain't a man alive can say what's truly right or mortal wrong when it comes to killing another man. General Bragg, he don't know. Miller Nalls, he don't know. Buck Burnet, he don't know. There ain't nobody knows. Not in this life."

Miller nodded and grew still. Alarmed, Buck whispered stridently, "Miller? You all right, Miller?"

The shaggy head moved in slowing response and Buck pressed him closer yet.

"Miller," he said, "you want to pray?"

"No," the other boy's voice was shallow but firm, "I already prayed, Buck. It was for you to come."

Buck looked down at him.

"You never did ask for much, did you?" he said softly.

But Miller only lay his head more deeply into the cradle of his friend's arm, smiled, sighed, and was gone. It was all the answer he ever gave Buck's question and all the answer the latter ever needed.

Five minutes later the roan stomped and made the warning chuckle in his throat again, and this time Buck could hear the men himself. They were up by the house getting off their horses.

"*Hoh, shuh,* be quiet, little horse," Buck called to the mustang. "I hear you but I can't do nothing about it."

Beyond the doorway a shadow loomed. Buck held his breath. Other shadows moved up, joining the first.

"Boys," called Wirt Rambeau, "don't do nothing foolish now. Come on out peaceful."

He waited, then raised his voice.

"If you're in there, boys, speak up."

Still nothing.

"Burnet," he said, 'we *know* you're in there. Craney's here with me. Call out, kid. Last chance."

By some atavistic instinct of survival Buck felt warned against answering. There came to him a wild hunted notion to hide, and in the darkness his eyes fell upon the feedbin. He staggered upward to raise the lid and slip under it into the bin. He fell forward into the well of sightless black within. He lit on something hot and rank of odor, and a barn rat the size of a young cat squealed beneath him and bit him savagely in the belly.

Buck slid his one hand under himself. The rat slashed at his hand, squealingly, and Buck closed his grip and strangled its entire body in one crushing fury of revulsion. Then he lay there, the musty filth of grain dust and rodent droppings choking his nostrils, the muscular evil body of the rat still convulsing like a furred snake in his hand.

Eternity passed. Then a muffled voice said, "What was that?" And another answered, "Sounded like a rat thumping under the floorboards." And a third man said, "Yes, it was. I heard him squeal."

Then it was Rambeau's voice saying tersely, "Light the lantern and stand by. Craney and me will go in alone."

"What the hell's the lantern for?" queried a trooper.

"So they will see we ain't up to nothing. Light it."

There was the scrape of a match, then the flare of the coal-oil wick being turned up.

Through a crack in his close-aired prison Buck could see the legs of Rambeau and Craney.

"There's my horse," he heard Craney say.

There followed a little stillness then, and Rambeau spoke with deliberate loudness.

"Yes, and there's his rider, yonder."

The legs moved over to stand by Miller Nalls.

"This is the big boy," said Craney. "The one Bragg wanted so bad. He's dead."

"Yes," said Rambeau, voice lowered now. "And *he* sure didn't ride that roan in here."

Craney dropped his voice, too.

"That leaves the Burnet kid," he said.

"It might," answered Rambeau still more guardedly, and Craney said quickly, "What you mean, it might?"

"I mean it would be all right with me if it left him."

"Yeah, yeah—maybe you're right."

Rambeau looked at him carefully and asked, "How about the horse? You want to leave him, too?"

Craney shrugged, letting his reply carry clearly. "Sure, leave the horse. The Provost Marshal's men can pick him up in the morning. I got a better one outside."

"All right," said Wirt Rambeau, "let's go."

They carried Miller Nalls outside and put him on the ground. The soldiers stared down at him.

"That all of them?" inquired one of the men.

"Others must have got on acrost the crick," said Rambeau.

"We going after them?" asked another man.

"I'm not," answered Rambeau. "I had orders to search a barn. I searched one."

"I dunno, Sarge," began a third trooper, but Rambeau cut him off.

"Bowen," he said, "you want to wander off in the dark looking for that Texas kid with the Navy pistol, you do it, hear? I got to get this other boy on down to Bragg at Tupelo."

"Hell," said the soldier, "I ain't lost no Texas kids with Navy pistols. What you want did with this one here?"

"Go up to that front shed and get them two mules," ordered Rambeau. "Hook them to that corn wagon in the yard. Bring a bedsheet out of the house and hurry it up. You and Bledsoe go."

Within minutes the wagon was brought down and Miller Nalls was lifted carefully into its narrow bed, the clean sheet wound properly about him. When he was in, Wirt Rambeau said, "Me and Craney will drive. Tie our horses onto the tailgate."

They climbed up. Rambeau settled his grip on the reins, clucked to his team. "Get along mules. It's a far, lonesome piece down the road to Tupelo."

They rode in silence for a considerable, thoughtful time. Rambeau dug out his pipe, lit it. Craney reached in his pocket for his plug, bit off a linted corner.

Rambeau looked around, judging the distance to the following soldiers, nodded, satisfied they were out of hearing.

"Craney," he said, "happen you was a betting man, how would you bet on that roan of yours being in that barn when the Provost Marshal's men go to look for him tomorrow morning?"

"You mean he might bust loose during the night, or something like that?"

"Yeah, something like that."

Craney thought it over. He shifted his cheekful of cut-plug, dappled the rump of the near mule, shook his head slowly.

"No takers," he said. "I wouldn't put nothing past a Texas

pony. I wouldn't even bet he's still in the barn right now."

Sergeant Wirt Rambeau nodded, drew deeply on his pipe. "You know something, Craney?" he exhaled with a certain sigh of final satisfaction. "Neither would I."

Tales of the West

For just 25 cents each, these action-packed Westerns are available at your favorite newsstands or by ordering directly from the publisher.

- [ ] **1984 SAVAGES, THE, Peter Dawson.** A brand-new novel of the old West and five brothers the whole country couldn't whip.

- [ ] **1977 TAGGART, Louis L' Amour.** A man who was always in trouble, should he stay and help her or get away to safety?

- [ ] **1949 GUNFIGHTER'S RETURN, Ben Smith.** He was on a mission of revenge. And his target was his own brother.

- [ ] **1934 OUTLAW, Frank Gruber.** The story of Jim Chapman who made his name a terror wherever railroads ran and banks did business.

- [ ] **1926 BARBED WIRE KINGDOM, C. William Harrison.** "Bob-wire", it raised hell all over the range, wherever it got strung up and now he was bringing it to his home range in Texas.

- [ ] **1925 SILENT RIVER, Wayne Roberts.** Along the wild Missouri, Lt. Endicott fought for his country, his life, his woman.

- [ ] **1916 AND THE WIND BLOWS FREE, Luke Short.** Big Jim Wade and his woman, a novel as savage as hungry Cheyennes on the warpath.

- [ ] **1905 FIRST FAST DRAW, THE, Louis L' Amour.** The blazing story of a man who learned he could live only by his skill with a gun.

- [ ] **1893 RIO BRAVO, Leigh Brackett.** Only three men stood up for the town when all hell broke loose!

- [ ] **1873 MODOC, THE LAST SUNDOWN, L. P. Holmes.** Brutal savage story of the last, courageous, defiant stand of the Modoc Indians against the power of the U.S. Army.

- [ ] **1866 SUMMER OF THE SMOKE, Luke Short.** Magnificent novel of white greed and brutality and of savage Indian reprisal.

- [ ] **1865 RAWHIDE AND BOB-WIRE, Luke Short.** Tales of the men and women who made the Old West.

- [ ] **1856 OUTLAW OF LONGBOW, THE, Peter Dawson.** He rode alone into the blazing guns that killed his brother . . .

- [ ] **1853 RADIGAN, Louis L'Amour.** A powerful and moving love story, a story of hard men in a harsh land.

- [ ] **1822 PLUNDERERS, THE, L. P. Holmes.** WATER—you had to have it, some shared it, some saved it, some killed for it.

- [ ] **1821 PLAY A LONE HAND, Luke Short.** Giff Dixon had to play it that way—the town the range and the man all belonged to the man who was trying to kill him.

- [ ] **1794 LAW BRINGERS, THE, William Porter.** They were closer than brothers but one believed in judges and juries—the other made his own law with a gun.

- [ ] **1769 LAND GRABBERS, THE, John S. Daniels.** They called him squaw-lover because he fought for the Indians.

- [ ] **1755 FIDDLEFOOT, Luke Short.** An explosive novel of a lazy, no-guts drifter—turned tough.

THE BEST SELLERS COME FROM BANTAM BOOKS!

BANTAM BOOKS, INC., Dept. K, 414 East Golf Rd., Des Plaines, Illinois.
Please send the Westerns which I have checked.

Name....................................... I enclose $...........plus 10c per

book for postage and handling.

Address.................................... (NOTE: On orders of more than 5

books there is NO postage charge.)

City........................Zone........ Check or Money Order—

NO CURRENCY PLEASE—Sorry, No

State...................................... C.O.D.'s.

K-11-62